RHODES'S REWARD

Heroes for Hire, Book 4

Dale Mayer

Books in This Series:

RHODES'S REWARD: HEROES FOR HIRE, BOOK 4
Dale Mayer
Valley Publishing

ISBN-13: 978-1-773360-31-7
Print Edition

Back Cover

Welcome *to Rhodes's Reward,* book 4 in Heroes for Hire, reconnecting readers with the unforgettable men from SEALs of Honor in a new series of action packed, page turning romantic suspense that fans have come to expect from USA TODAY Bestselling author Dale Mayer.

Second chances do happen... Even amid evil...

Rhodes knew Sienna years ago. When she'd been young and gawky, more elbow and carrot hair than style, but she'd had something special even then. Now she's all grown. But she's a trouble magnet, and even at the compound it finds her...

Sienna had a super-sized crush on her brother's best friend years ago. Now he's hunky and even hotter than she could have imagined. Only she's new and doesn't want to jeopardize her position. When asked to help out on a job, she agrees...and triggers a sequence of disastrous events no one could foresee.

But someone will stop at nothing to silence everyone involved, especially the two of them...

Sign up to be notified of all Dale's releases here!

http://dalemayer.com/category/blog/

Chapter 1

A SHIT JOB. A shit trip. A shit deal.

But he was home. Thank God.

Tired and haggard, Rhodes Gorman walked in the front door and headed straight for his suite on the second floor. He opened the door to his bedroom, dumped his bags and collapsed fully on his bed. He didn't bother undressing, and the thought of a shower was a lot more than he could handle right now. He closed his eyes to let the world take him away.

But instead his mind filled with the scenes and pain of the last few days. He and Harrison had gone overseas, tracking down a person with some intel. Now they were both home, but it hadn't been an easy job and the trip back—brutal. But they'd made it, and all he needed now was a chance to sleep.

Even with his door closed, he could still hear other people in the main house, the voices filtering through his head. One male. One female. Ice used to be the only female in the group, but that was rapidly changing. In his tired mode Rhodes couldn't understand or identify who that female was. Until she spoke again. Sienna. So she was still here. Good. Saved him a trip to haul her back again. They had unfinished business, whether she knew it or not.

"Why would you want to stay here?" asked the guy.

Who was that? Rhodes wondered.

"Because it's different. I feel safe here, "Sienna said. "I like the people." Her voice had shifted there—softening. "I enjoy the work."

"Safe?"

Yeah, that word caught Rhodes's interest too. But the change in tone at the word *people* was something else altogether.

"Yes, even though the compound has been attacked twice," she said, "everybody handled it so well. It was just like military clockwork."

"That's because it was," the man said.

Whoever the man was, he had influence over Sienna, and from the way she talked to him, she obviously knew him well. There was respect and familiarity in her tone ... and love. Rhodes frowned. Who the hell was this guy? Jealously crept in.

"Jarrod, you can't rule my life."

Rhodes's eyes flew open. Jarrod? Jarrod Bentley, Rhodes's navy buddy was here? He'd been gone for two different four-week tours overseas. Planned to come by here each time he returned to the States. The first time he'd talked Sienna into leaving with him. But he was not fully informed. Rhodes heard she was just tying up loose ends to move here. Permanently. Figured Jarrod had come back while Rhodes was gone. Slowly he sat up, his head cocked to better hear the conversation out in the hallway.

He had met Sienna years ago, since he and Jarrod were brother SEALs. But he hadn't recognized her when she first came to the compound. Maybe because she had been a pimply face, awkward-arms-and-legs, bony-knees-and-elbows gangly teenager back then. Not the striking beauty who'd walked into the house with Ice that day. Even though she had said she was Jarrod's sister, he really hadn't made the connection. Not until hours later when he'd caught sight of that long-ago teenager inside the beautiful woman.

And then he didn't know how to bring up their earlier meeting. He'd never forgotten her. In fact, Jarrod had warned him away back then, already seeing Rhodes's interest, but who knew she'd turn out to be such a beauty?

Between the two attacks on the compound, the op in Afghanistan—rescuing Lissa—and then a series of jobs covering for Merk while he was busy protecting his ladylove, Rhodes had been more than a little busy.

With Sienna here, there's no way he would sleep now. Plus he didn't want to miss out on seeing his old friend, Jarrod. Rhodes sat up, then stood, stripped and stepped into the shower.

Soaking under the hot water gave him a sense of renewal. When he was done, he quickly dressed.

Nobody was in the hallway when he walked out. At the kitchen, he stopped to see Alfred and found him pouring a cup of coffee, which he handed to Rhodes. "I didn't know if you would choose a shower and some food or just sleep."

"I tried sleeping. That didn't work so well," he joked. "I figured coffee and some grub would hit the spot." He glanced around. "Did I hear Jarrod's voice?"

Alfred nodded. "Jarrod is indeed here. He came back to check on his sister."

"Rhodes?" The man's voice came from behind him.

Rhodes spun, and sure enough there was Jarrod. The huge carrot top had been a new recruit when Rhodes had joined Levi's SEAL unit. For some reason Jarrod and Rhodes had become great friends. He put down his cup and greeted his long-time buddy. "What the hell? I go away and come back to find you're trying to step into my place."

"Not quite," Jarrod said with a smile. "Although Levi has made it very clear there's a spot here, if I ever need it."

"Damn, that would be great." As Rhodes studied his friend's face, he realized Jarrod wasn't quite ready to make that change yet. "Being a SEAL is the best, but there comes a time ... not many make it past ten years."

"Understood." Jarrod nodded. "It's always in the back of my mind, just not yet."

"Who knows? Maybe Levi will open a second compound on the West Coast. We certainly end up crossing to that side a lot to handle business. We almost have enough to keep us there full time."

Jarrod's eyebrows rose. "You guys are that busy?"

Rhodes nodded. "I just got back from one overseas. After I've had a bit of a rest and get filled back up, I'll be bugging Levi to get me out of here again."

"Who knew?" Jarrod shook his head.

"The world's in bad shape right now," Rhodes said soberly.

"What kind of work are you doing mostly? Hate to think of becoming nothing more than a glorified bodyguard."

"Some of it's foreign security stuff, and then there's all the private kind for the elite. Ex-princes. Billionaires. Dot.com geeks. We do a lot of domestic work."

"Any military stuff?" Jarrod asked.

"None that's ever spoken about publicly." Rhodes studied his friend. "Let's just say we haven't lost all ties."

He realized that had been the right thing to say because Jarrod's face lit up. He'd been a military man since forever, and it was really hard to walk away from that lifestyle. When one took pride in defending his country, everything else paled in comparison. But if Jarrod knew he would be able to do the same thing he was already doing, there was a chance he would join them. Rhodes motioned toward the long table in front of him and said, "Have a coffee with me and tell me what's going on with your sister. How the hell did she end up here anyway?"

Jarrod shook his head. "I still don't know, even after my first visit here. I thought she was safe and sound at home. Next thing I know, Levi's texting and saying Ice brought her into the compound."

"It's what any of us would do," Rhodes said quietly. "We might have helped her initially, but she stayed because she's good at what she does. Ice and Levi wouldn't allow anything less. And Alfred, I'm sure he's run her ragged, testing her in ways she didn't know."

Jarrod grinned. "Yeah, she doesn't quite get all that."

"If she can do what she does and handle living here with us, then she's got to be an angel."

"If she is, I didn't see it growing up." Jarrod chuckled. "No, that's not quite true. She was just so different. We treated her like a china doll because we didn't know what else to do with the only sister to four brothers. We were afraid she'd break."

Rhodes smirked. "I don't think that treatment here will work. She wouldn't appreciate it."

"No, I wouldn't," said Sienna from the doorway, her tone exasperated and a little too loud. She sat down on the bench beside her brother, literally bumping against him and saying, "Move over."

Jarrod gave a shout of laughter and nodded his head at Rhodes. "We might want to treat her as a china doll, but she

5

won't let us."

Rhodes studied them, seeing the same closeness he'd noted a long time ago. "I met you way back when, you know?"

She shot him a shuttered look and nodded. "I remember."

"I didn't at first," Rhodes said in confession. "Besides, you've changed a lot," he said in an admiring tone. "You used to be this gangly teenager—all elbows, knees and freckles, with red hair going everywhere."

Jarrod snorted. "She still is." But he wrapped an arm around her shoulder and hugged her close. "Now, if she would stop being so damn independent and let us know when she gets into trouble, it'd make us all happy."

"You're always so busy," she said quietly. "Besides it wasn't anything I couldn't handle."

Jarrod turned to her and, in a much harder voice, said, "Ice found you at the gas station with a backpack, sitting under a tree, lost. You had no place to go. You were out of money and had no wheels. How was that 'handling' the issue? The least you could have done was call. We would've been happy to help."

She stared at the table but didn't answer.

Rhodes understood. Independence was a hard battle. When life beat you down, you didn't want anyone to know.

"At least Ice was the one who found Sienna," Rhodes said calmly. "We're not axe murderers. Once she got here, we were quite happy to invite her to stay."

Other thoughts rippled in his head, but to add more was taking the chance he would just piss her off. She shot him a grateful look, and he realized he'd said the right thing. A good thing. He glanced at Jarrod and got a nod of approval from him too. Rhodes sighed. This family stuff was rough. He was an only child, and his parents had retired to Tucson, Arizona where they liked to do morning brunch beside the pool with the rest of the retirees who lived in the complex and then play Scrabble and other board games in the evening. They were happy, so he was too. He'd been a very late-in-life child for them, and his decision to join the military was one they both approved of. He didn't see them very much, but called them often.

"Besides, Sienna has taken over the office work. And if you try to take her away from us, Stone may have something to say."

"Stone?" Jarrod asked with a frown.

"Yes, office work was his punishment whenever he pushed his recovery too much. We're always building new prototypes for that leg of his. Somehow he'd keep his stump more or less sored up. And that meant office work—and a lot of it."

Jarrod gave a subtle laugh. "I keep forgetting he's missing a leg. He's adapted so well," he said in admiration.

"It was a hard adjustment," Rhodes said in a low voice. "He never let anybody know, but it wasn't easy on him."

Jarrod nodded. "I don't imagine it would be." He studied Rhodes's face. "And you're okay? I heard the whole unit got blown up. But when I realized you were all ambulatory and then created this company together, I figured you were fine."

Rhodes said, "I'm fine now. Merk and I were injured but not anywhere near as badly as the other two. For us it was a couple broken bones. We were in traction for a while, lots of soft tissue damage, bruises on the liver, things like that."

"Sounds horrible," Sienna said.

Rhodes caught Sienna's sympathetic look. He quickly turned away. Sympathy was the last thing he wanted. Although his gaze kept straying back toward her, he realized he deserved a special reward for keeping his hands to himself. Because dammit she was hot.

He swallowed hard and turned as Alfred walked in at the right moment, carrying a plate of roast beef, gravy, and veggies and put it down in front of Rhodes.

"Alfred, this looks delicious," he said in relief. "I didn't realize how hungry I was until now."

"Just leftovers. They all had it last night."

"Wow, they actually left me some?" But he was already busy with his knife and fork, cutting into the moist tender meat. He put the first bite in his mouth and closed his eyes as he chewed. "Oh, my God, this is so good."

Jarrod said, his voice envious, "You guys are so lucky to have Alfred." He turned to his sister and said, "So that's the real reason you want to stay here."

Sienna laughed. "Alfred is a dream. If he were thirty years younger, I'd consider going after him myself."

Rhodes smirked. "Do you think we haven't thought of that? I don't twist that way, but I might consider it for a man who can cook like this. … *Hmm-hmm.*"

SOMETHING WAS JUST so damn attractive about a man who enjoyed his food. But he wasn't *eating*; he was savoring every bite. Rhodes had come to her house a couple times with Jarrod way back when. Once, when Sienna had lived with her brother, Rhodes had spent five days at their place. She hadn't taken her eyes off that big tough badass male. And yet he'd never once made her afraid.

In fact, the longer he'd stayed, the more she'd followed him around just to be in his presence. He oozed confidence and power. Back then, she'd felt ugly and awkward. To make it worse, she'd been fascinated by him but clueless as how to deal with it. Now, of course, she understood so much more.

They were both adults, free of relationships and living in the same place.

She couldn't help but consider it. She again dropped her gaze to the table and played with the coffee cup in front of her. Odd to realize that, after all these years, the attraction was even stronger. She daren't let Jarrod know because he'd fight tooth and nail to keep her away from Rhodes if that's what she was staying for.

And Rhodes was only a small part of it, though he definitely factored into it. No way would he seek her out if she left. But while she was here, she could see if there was something to the attraction or not. She needed time to let Rhodes get past that code of honor that said friends' little sisters were out of bounds. And Rhodes was the kind of guy who would see his good behavior as part of his honor system. Unlike a lot of men who would look upon her as prey, Rhodes would see her as untouchable, someone to protect while her brother wasn't here.

A tiny smile played at the corner of her mouth. Or maybe it wouldn't be an issue … if he found something he wanted badly enough.

"You okay, Sienna?"

She stopped and turned toward Jarrod. "Sorry, was lost in my thoughts for a moment there." She stared directly into her brother's eyes, knowing perfectly well that if she didn't pass this test, her life could get very difficult.

He searched her gaze for a long moment, then as if satisfied, he turned back to Rhodes. "So catch me up on your ops over the last year," he said.

Sienna sat quietly and listened to the two men share the events they'd gone through over the past twelve months. She wanted to hear as much as she could, but at the same time, she had work to do. Sienna stood up, patted her brother on the shoulder and said, "I'm not sure when you're leaving, but I have to get back to the office."

He reached out and caught her hand and said, "I leave in the morning."

She bent down, kissed him on the cheek and gave him a quick hug. She stepped away and tossed back, "I'll let you two old ladies sit here and gossip." She smiled at Alfred as she filled up her coffee cup, then headed to the office.

She still didn't understand everything that went on at Legendary Security, but she was starting to. Her first few days here had been hairy, but it had given her an interesting insight. Initially it had been unnerving, wondering what she had gotten herself into and with whom, but then she quickly realized how much and how well they took care of not just her but the entire place.

And how similar they all were to her brothers.

There was a certain freedom in being here. In an odd way she hadn't been free for a long time. She'd also met a kindred spirit here—Katina, Merk's partner, who was also an accountant. Not a programmer like Sienna was, but still Katina understood the financial world. And she'd been to hell and back herself.

In Sienna's case it wasn't her job that had done her in, but the people around her. She'd worked for an independent contractor looking into a series of banking irregularities inside the programming, hackers stealing within the system.

Very detailed work. And a special niche career.

She found what she thought was proof and handed it over but hadn't realized that her lover was part of the same criminal organization. When things had blown up, and the dust had settled, she'd been blamed for all kinds of things, like sleeping with the enemy. She'd lost everything, including her good name.

She'd walked away and started fresh.

Now nobody knew who she was, what she'd done, and where she'd gone. She told Jarrod some of it, but outside of it being a bad deal, there was no going back.

In fact, compared to what Lissa and Katina had been through, Sienna's life was bland and boring. Sure, she'd lost her job and had been betrayed by her lover, and was pretty damn sure her boss had been involved in the whole deal too, but all that was mild when compared to their lives.

Back in the office she settled down at her desk, pulled out her cell and checked the time. She was surprised it was so late already. She buckled down and started on the bookkeeping.

Compared to what she used to do, this was incredibly simple. But the mindlessness of it was also a joy. She didn't have to study lines of endless code or worry and fret over patterns she could see but not yet understand. She was fine not having to dig and follow trails and puzzles in order to ferret out the information needed. No subterfuge was here, and that alone was a relief. When her phone rang an hour later, she didn't think anything of it. She picked it up and answered, "Hello?"

"Sienna?"

"Yes, who's this?

"Bullard."

She sat back with a grin. "Hey, Bullard. Normally you don't call me directly."

"Nope, I don't. But this time I have a question for you."

"What's up?" She tossed down her pencil, leaning back in her chair. She liked Bullard, from the little bit she'd seen of him. He planned on coming back soon. She looked forward to that.

"You used to troubleshoot financial systems—banking software, accounting discrepancies—didn't you?" His voice gentled. "I remember Levi mentioning something like that."

She frowned. "I *used* to do something like that," she said. "I don't anymore."

"Any reason why?"

"Yeah, it didn't work out so well," she said in a dry tone. "Sometimes keeping your nose clean is better than digging for dirt."

He gave a bellowing laugh. "So true. But the business we're in doesn't keep our noses very clean. If I sent you some files, could you tell me where they're from?"

"Not necessarily," she said with a frown. "What type of files? And what do they have to do with my skills?"

"It's a little bit confusing. A friend, part owner of an African bank in Ghana, has found some discrepancies in their accounting. He has someone in mind who could be responsible, only that employee's son has worked with them for about a year as well, and both family members make up their IT department, doing all the upgrades and tweaks to the banking software. So he's reticent to have those guys look at the problem in case they are involved. He sent us access to the back end and several sheets found in the old man's desk. Only my computer specialist isn't accessible, and we aren't making heads or tails out of this."

In spite of herself she was intrigued. Impulsively she said, "Feel free to email them to me, but that doesn't mean I'll help."

"Done," he said triumphantly.

She rolled her eyebrows as she realized the email sat in her inbox, staring at her. "Is this something Levi knows about?"

"He's been giving me a hand on this case."

She nodded. "In that case, I'll look."

"Can you do that while I'm on the line?" he asked hopefully.

She double-clicked on the email and then opened the attachment. Instantly the lines of code appeared. She leaned forward to study it. "Do I get any contextual reference?" she said with a laugh. "This means nothing with so little."

"Money, drugs, and/or weapons," he said succinctly. "We think money is siphoned from a bank here in Africa, then transferred into a US account, where it's used for drug deals and buying weapons—to ship possibly back over here again. The trail led to Dallas."

"Oh." She winced.

She studied the figures, rapidly scanning the columns, her mind quickly interpreting the data. "Okay, so these are from the back end of a banking program. They are transactions, but very little information is here."

Silence came first. "Wow. That was fast."

"Fast but useless," she said cheerfully. "You need more data than this, a lot more."

"Did you check the second attachment?"

She quickly opened and scrolled down to see a PDF of spreadsheets, potentially from a ledger book. What he'd given her was just a drop of water in a missing lake of knowledge. She took a couple minutes to assimilate the information, then said, "I need so much more, preferably the program itself."

"It's all about the gold standard."

She returned her attention to the code. "Right, I can see it now." Indeed, on the last page she found one of the identifying banks, a small regional bank in Ghana. She continued to peruse that line of code. "This is old COBOL code. With a lot of updates …" Her voice petered off as she studied the subsequent lines of code. "Interesting. It's quite an antiquated system. I've seen a lot similar to this, but still wince every time I find some."

"Wow, again so fast. No wonder Levi hired you."

"No, he doesn't really know I can do this type of work." She laughed. "My skills are not a highly prized skill set in the world of private security companies."

"You'd be surprised. But for Levi's company, he's more interested in security on the human level. Mine on the other hand, is more interested in software security. So, any programmer who can see what and how code has been hacked, … that's worth a lot."

She shook her head, even though he couldn't see it. "Nah, I'm sure your guys would've figured this out. I might've gotten it in ten minutes, but they would've in twenty."

Bullard laughed. "We've had it for hours and had no idea what we were looking at." He added, "If you find anything else, please give me a ring back."

"The snippets aren't enough if you want me to see exact-ly what the developer has done," she said. "I'll need full access."

"Not sure that's possible. My guy sent me several videos

of code streaming. I can send that to you. What we're really looking for is a connection to the spreadsheets and some explanation as to what they mean." He quickly said good-bye and hung up.

She studied the sheets on the screen but really needed them as a hard copy, so she clicked on the correct icon and pulled them from the printer. She wanted to study the code, but had her own work to finish first.

She settled back to her usual job. She had tons of bookkeeping transactions to enter and then papers to file. By the time she was done, she felt like she'd accomplished something.

Levi stepped into the room as she put away folders. She glanced at him and said, "Bullard called and asked me to look at some code snippets he had for a banking scheme."

"Good. I told him you might help."

"I just printed the sheets off, actually." She pointed to them on the side table. "But they are nothing that I need."

He looked at them. "He sent them to me too."

She finished clearing off her desk and said, "I'm putting in a shorter day because Jarrod's here."

Levi waved a hand at her. "I don't care how short your day is. When the work's done, it's done."

She laughed. "In this job the work is never done. There's always something for tomorrow." She quickly told Levi what she'd said to Bullard. She liked the way Levi's eyebrows shot up and how he studied the pages, as if seeing what she said. He'd have to know programming for that. But with Levi, who knew the extent of his knowledge. He might understand a dozen languages—even computer ones.

"Nice."

Bullard's email came in just then with more attachments. She quickly opened the first and clicked on the video. Instead code streamed on her monitor. Her gaze danced across letters and numbers she was very familiar with. She opened up the other two, both shorter.

"Interesting." Levi studied the monitors behind her. "Does the code mean anything to you?"

"Maybe," she said, her focus intense, all three videos running at the same time.

She sat back and pursed her lips. She could see the transactions running through the code and accounts, but at the moment, it meant nothing to her. At least not yet.

"We'll be late for Alfred's dinner if we don't get going." She grabbed up the sheets and stacked them on her desk. They would take a lot longer. While the remnants of code still whispered through the back of her brain, she headed to the doorway.

"I'm right with you." Together they walked downstairs. "Are you okay that Jarrod visits?" Levi asked. "With the two attacks here on the compound, it's natural for all of us to call family when someone could be in trouble."

She gave him a shuttered look. "Yet—twice—nobody considered asking me beforehand."

He grinned. "That's family. It often takes somebody else to point out what we should've done in the first place."

She rolled her eyes at him, stepped into the dining room and sat down at the table. Jarrod came in with a bunch of the other men, taking a spot beside her. Instantly the room filled with boisterous conversation. Once Alfred carried in platters of food, the conversation slowed down. She caught Rhodes eyeing the roast pork coming his way and smiled. He looked like he planned on having the whole thing.

She glanced around the room, unable to hold in her

smile. How lucky that she'd landed here. She could have ended up so many other places. But Ice had been a godsend. Sienna focused on the table and served herself some food—and froze. She slowly raised her head to stare out the window on the far side. There was just something about one of those lines of code, … and now she understood.

With her mind spinning, she realized something else. She'd seen similar entries in one of the classic textbook cases she'd been taught years ago. She pulled out her phone and quickly hit Redial on Bullard's number.

"It's Sienna. The program is converting currencies and rounding them up and down. I won't know for sure unless I have access to the entire system, but at a guess, I'd say the fractional differences were moved to a third account. Fractions of a cent add up damn quick and are almost impossible to trace like this."

The entire room froze, and maybe she shouldn't have made the call in the dining room. She lifted her gaze and caught sight of Rhodes. He frowned at her.

But Levi leaned across the table and said in a hard voice, "Sienna, are you sure?"

Slowly, she nodded her head, hearing Bullard's exclamation on the other end. She answered, "I'm as sure as I can be without having access to the program. But a developer would be doing this. The code is robust but antiquated. A programmer would need to know COBOL and the more modern languages. It's been heavily upgraded and patched but still based on that system."

"Why is that?" Rhodes asked.

"Because it's too expensive for most institutions to change from the original, and as it is robust, it's a great foundation block. Then, like any old infrastructure, it needs updating, debugging, and constant testing. Myriad third-party products support these issues, but again you need a good developer who understands COBOL in the first place. Or several, depending on the size of the bank, the job done originally, and the maintenance." She glanced around the table. "Whoever is doing the tweaks on their end, chances are he's older and looking for a way to retire. And he's likely been doing this for a long time ..." She added, "He's not making much off the system initially but over time ..."

"Oh, very nice," Bullard said. "I'll be in touch with the bank and get back to you."

"Wait," she cried. "I haven't looked at the spreadsheets yet. I don't understand the connection to the code."

"Maybe there isn't one, but we're hoping so." He chuckled. "After this I'm expecting great things from you." And just as quickly he was gone.

She groaned. "Great."

But she got no help from the others. They were too busy grinning at her.

Chapter 2

SIENNA WOKE THE next morning tired and achy. Instead of enjoying a peaceful dinner last night, the place had erupted with questions and phone calls. She hadn't meant to create such a stir, but when she had connected the sequences in her head, she realized she could look at them in a completely different way. And apparently, that made a difference. She still had to study the spreadsheets …

The group had discussed the issue at length even though she'd said, "I could be wrong."

"But you could also be very right," Jarrod said, sounding impressed. "I didn't know that was the kind of work you did."

"I was doing all kinds." She smiled at him. "It was fun until it blew up in my face."

"Time to tell me exactly what went wrong," Jarrod said in a hard voice.

"It's over." She shrugged. "What difference does it make?"

Katina reached across the table and covered her hand. "I've been there, and it sucks," she said. "But it's much better if these guys know exactly what happened to you in the past."

Sienna frowned. "It's just so … embarrassing." The last thing she wanted was to air her dirty laundry in front of anybody else.

"Give."

Her brother had always been like that. One to bark out orders and expect her to follow. She glared at him. But his expression never eased. She threw up her hands and said, "Fine, I was part of a criminal investigation into a leg of the Mafia. Hard to believe they're around, but they are."

Katina gasped in horror.

"Anyway, while I was looking in the banking transactions to prove they were involved in money laundering, I didn't realize who and what they were after until finding all the information. And my current boyfriend at that time was actually part of the Mafia family." She winced. "It all went south. My bosses said I was sleeping with the enemy, that my information was tainted, so the case was thrown out. I lost my job and good name." She glared at everybody. "Embarrassing enough?"

Jarrod reached over and grabbed her hand, tugging her into his arms for a hug. "You didn't know who he was. That's a heavy weight you had on your shoulders."

When he released her, she said, "Everybody just likes to have a scapegoat. I was it. The stupid thing is, I'm pretty damn sure my boss was part of the same family. I think I was given that job specifically because I was in a position that would compromise the case."

She fisted both hands and stretched them back out again to make them relax. "But it really makes you reassess who you can trust in this world."

"And there is not one person at this table who has not already had to reassess that exact same issue," Jarrod said quietly.

"We were all betrayed by somebody we trusted," Rhodes

said. "Maybe we were foolish to trust in the first place. For some of us, the betrayal was more serious than for others." Rhodes shook his head. "It's a hard lesson to learn but better to know."

"Did you go to the police and report what they did to you?" Katina asked Sienna.

"The police were all over me by that time. I'm lucky I wasn't charged," she said in a low voice. "There was talk of it. Only because I gave as much evidence as I could, was I able to walk away. As it is right now, everybody walked, because whatever I found was supposedly tainted." She lifted her gaze and said, "It was pretty humiliating at the time. I felt so stupid. I had no idea my boyfriend was involved."

Katina patted her hand. "And it doesn't matter. That's all in your past. Time to face forward and forget about him." She gave a lopsided smile. "These guys are good at helping you do that." She linked her arm with Merk. "Merk helped me out of my jam."

"Nobody can help me out of mine," Sienna said. "It's done and gone. The aftermath was pretty rough, and the fallout was terrible. I would have kept falling, but Ice found me, and I am very thankful for that," she admitted. "I couldn't do anything to undo it, so I just moved forward," Sienna said. "We've all come to crossroads in our lives where what we used to do isn't what we currently do." She shrugged. "Honestly, I'm going to enjoy my new life."

Levi wrapped an arm around Ice's shoulder, tucking her close.

Sienna could certainly understand why Ice was happy. As much as Sienna hoped for the same, she wasn't at all sure it would happen.

Abruptly Levi asked, "Did you like that kind of work?"

"Yes," she said. "I did. It was fun to chase the trails. Sometimes it was also frustrating because it would just end, and I had nowhere to go. I had to wait until something else happened. But often I could keep tracking and find out more."

"I have to admit, I would've enjoyed going farther into that field myself," Katina said. "The little bit I got involved with was interesting, but also unnerving."

"If it was directed at you, then it would definitely be. But I was going after criminals—at least I thought I was." Sienna shook her head. "I'm honestly not sure who I was chasing now. Because if my boss was involved, … who knows." She turned to gaze at Levi and realized he was studying her thoughtfully. "What are you thinking?"

"Sometimes we get asked to look in to things like that," he said. "I haven't had anybody I could put onto cases involving that level of programming before now. Money trails we've looked in to tended toward offshore accounts. Certain ones can be very time-consuming. I'm wondering if it's something you want to get away from completely or would like to get further into."

She hesitated a moment. "I'm not sure that's what I could do. I specialized in banking programs. I'd have to know that it was completely legal before I would venture into it again. I got off lightly, considering. Not sure the law would let me go so easily a second time."

"And yet you helped out Bullard," Ice said.

Sienna's lips twisted. "Yeah, he caught me in a weak moment. He's very persuasive."

At that Ice laughed out loud. "Oh, he is indeed. He also has a greater variety of work and would have more exposure to cases like this."

"I'd be fine as long as it wasn't something I'd end up in trouble over," she said finally. "That part wasn't fun."

"I so understand." Katina laughed. "Like you, I don't want to end up in something that is dangerous. I was already kidnapped and someone tried to kill me over the mess I got involved in."

Sienna's gaze widened. "Oh, my situation wasn't anywhere near that bad. I can't imagine what you went through."

"Well," Merk added, "you may not have known how bad it was because you were the one set up to take the fall. In this case, Katina wanted the others to." Merk's explanation brought a laugh from everyone.

"I wish I'd thought of that, but I didn't even see the danger closing in around me," Sienna said. "I don't think like that. I thought I was a happy-go-lucky person, and pretty intuitive. Only I didn't really know the kind of people I was working with. I'd never come up against individuals like that before."

"How long were you with your boyfriend before this all came apart?" Katina asked.

Sienna hugged her coffee mug. "Honestly, not long. I can see now he set me up, targeted me. He'd probably researched me beforehand, so he knew what I liked, what buttons to push. It was a pretty fast whirlwind romance. About three months, maybe four, that I'd known him."

Rhodes nodded. "That sounds like about the right time frame. A con of that magnitude would require at least three months to set up. Obviously, they had enough in place for you to take the fall."

"Doesn't matter anyway," she said. "My reputation's in tatters, and I certainly won't be working in that field anymore."

"Unless you want to do that kind of work for me," Levi said. "I already know how the story played out and understand."

And she had no doubt he meant it. "Why don't we leave it at that? If you get something across your desk that might involve matters like this, I could look." But she didn't really expect anything to come of it.

Until the next morning when Bullard called her again. "I have another bit of code for you to look at."

She leaned back in her chair, rubbing her temple. "Have you talked to Levi about this?"

He laughed. "Of course I have. Levi and I are working on the case jointly."

There really was something magnetic about that voice of his. But she was immune to smooth talkers. "Okay, send it over."

She hung up and returned to the accounts she was setting up for the business. Levi had done a decent job, but some fine-tuning would make it work that much better. She was busy with the forms when an email alert sounded. She checked and saw Bullard had sent four more videos. He really wanted answers.

She downloaded the videos and brought them up on the double monitors. She split the screens so all four played at the same time. All codes were again similar to what she had looked at the day before. She read them over, but at first glance, they didn't appear to mean much. Same program but with newer updates. She studied the stream for close to half an hour.

Levi walked in. "Are those Bullard's files?"

Without lifting her head, she said, "Yes."

"Okay. How about letting Katina help? She has quite a photographic memory. It's one of the reasons she was so instrumental in putting the company she was working for behind bars. When she found access to information, she memorized the material."

Sienna looked up at him in surprise. "You know, that could be very helpful." She motioned at the fourth video and said, "This is different."

He stepped over to stand behind her. "Different how?"

"The others are all very similar to the first ones he showed me. This set of code is replicating, so everything it does, it does twice. Like a mirror image."

She minimized the other videos and opened the fourth in full size. "It's not active. It's like a copy."

"Why?"

She shook her head. "I don't know, unless they are making changes, yet wanting to keep a master. They appear to be working on the code, but I can't see the extent of the tampering."

He tapped a finger on the far column and said, "Good. Bullard can go back to the bank and tell them that."

"Good." She smiled. "If that's all then ..."

"Can you track who is doing this?"

"Maybe. But not from here. And Ghana has their own specialists. Didn't he say there was a Dallas connection?"

He stepped away from the desk and said, "Looks like it. They're waiting on results from the bank investigation."

She nodded, but her gaze was still on the monitors. She heard Levi leave as quietly as he had appeared. She quickly brought up several of the programs she formerly used to hunt through databases. She'd caught glimpses of accounts. *Would it help to know what the transactions were?* She'd spent a lot of time doing this before. Very quickly she picked out one of the Swiss banks. Of course that made it even more difficult because those were much harder to get information from.

She kept digging and found several were running through France, and others through Hong Kong. She focused on the latter. Of course, a lot of offshore accounts ran through Asia.

RHODES AND MERK looked up when Levi walked into the kitchen. "What's up?"

"Bullard sent Sienna several videos tracing code from a different bank. She thinks the code has been tampered with."

"Is this Bullard's case or ours?" Rhodes asked.

"Both. There is a Dallas connection here."

"Wow, a shared job. That'll be a first."

"True, but it's good for both of us. Bullard has a lot of work over there, and we have a lot of over here, but obviously, if we can pull our resources on some jobs, it's major. He's also asking how the new security systems he installed are working. Anybody have any criticism or questions on them?"

Rhodes watched as Merk shook his head. "It's fine at the moment," he said. "Until it's put to the test, we can't know how the complete system works."

"I was kind of hoping not to have to stress it that bad." Levi sat down at the table and said, "Logan and Flynn are taking on a West Coast job. We have a couple special people to be escorted back to Texas, with any luck we'll be out and back faster than expected."

Rhodes nodded. "Anything from here I can help with?"

Levi glanced at the two of them. "Bored?"

Merk nodded.

"Bored," Rhodes confirmed. He wasn't so much bored as preferring a way to get out of the house while Sienna was here. Since Jarrod left, Rhodes saw himself in the brother role. And that wasn't the relationship he wanted. A break would be good.

"Bullard has located five addresses," Levi said. "One in New Mexico, four in Texas, the farthest up in Dallas."

"Addresses regarding what?" Rhodes asked.

"Connected to the banking fraud case Sienna is looking at right now," Levi said. "Several Texas addresses were on a sheet found on a bank employee's desk. Check out each one very carefully. Approach with caution, but we must confirm if these are safe houses, terrorists' hideouts, or just holding properties."

"Exactly what kind of a case has Bullard got going on?" Merk asked.

Levi looked up and said, "Arms dealing and money laundering. Plus, it looks like a bank employee might have been pilfering a bit off the top. At least if Sienna is correct. Who knows what else."

Rhodes's face went on lockdown. "Like hell. Sienna shouldn't be working on anything to do with that." Then he stopped himself. In the office, work was a hell of a lot less dangerous than being out in the field. She'd be safe here. He stood up. "I'm in."

Merk said, "Me too."

Rhodes asked Levi, "Driving or flying?"

"Driving." Levi stood up and walked out the kitchen. "Be ready to leave in an hour."

Merk and Rhodes looked at each other and smiled. "I guess he knew our answers already," Merk said.

"It's sure better than doing security detail," Rhodes said,

heartfelt. "He's been getting a lot of requests by these West Coast entertainers."

"Hell, I've had enough of that. He needs to hire guys just for that babysitting stuff if that's what he's doing now. It's probably very lucrative and could keep the company in ready cash while we do the other jobs." Merk rapped his knuckles against the kitchen table and said, "Meet you back here in forty-five."

Rhodes headed up to his suite, happy to leave again. He'd just worry about Sienna if he stayed here. Packing for him was a five-minute job. Too many years being ready to leave at the drop of a hat for him to live any other way. He was back down in thirty, walking into the kitchen to see Alfred had a picnic basket half-full already. "Alfred, you are a godsend."

"Yep, don't you forget it." Alfred quickly added home-made cookies and banana bread in clear plastic containers and then tucked in several large thermoses. "I suspect you both won't be more than two nights, and you'll be stopping at hotels anyway, so this should do you for the bulk of the trip."

Rhodes picked it up, grabbed his own bag and headed out to the truck. Considering the mileage they had to cover, he figured the smallest of the trucks would be easier on gas.

Merk already had the same idea as he had it warming up. He nodded at Rhodes. "Throw your bags in the back. Ice is bringing us the paperwork, and then we're gone."

Rhodes loaded the basket into the small back storage compartment of the extra cab and tossed his own bag in the back of the bed. It was a nice sunny day. No reason not to haul the luggage outside. Within minutes they were off. He checked the GPS. "It looks like we're three hours to the first address."

"Did you hear any whispers as to what might be there?" Merk asked.

Rhodes brought up his cell and punched in the address. He also checked the notes Levi had sent. Each location was registered to a different name. But as they had checked farther back, each had been under one company.

WHEN THEY PULLED onto the street of the first house, they drove past it slowly. It was a rundown large brick two-story house, comparable to the rest of the block. Nothing untoward, nor odd looking. An abandoned-looking vehicle was parked in the driveway. An alleyway was down the back.

Rhodes carefully drove to the rear and parked just behind the house. Merke and Rhodes got out and walked the alleyway carefully. Merk took several pictures of the area and this part of the house.

As he took the second one, Rhodes saw a curtain pull back and then quickly fall away again. "Somebody's in the top second room," he said to Merk.

Merk nodded. "I'll go around front and see if our presence here has pushed anybody out the door."

Rhodes nodded as he headed in the opposite direction to the neighboring house. From his view, the derelict-looking house appeared empty. He quickly hopped the fence and ran up to the back so he could peer at the house from the relative safety of this one. But with nothing showing as out-of-place or unusual, he continued around to the front.

He took several photos from this viewpoint. No windows were on this side. He quickly slipped through the hedge and crept up to peer around the front. Just as he caught sight of the car in the driveway, the engine turned over, and it immediately backed down to the street and took off away from Rhodes.

He caught sight of Merk at the far end of the driveway. As the car drove past, Merk turned and quickly snapped a photo. With any luck he got the license plate. They should have grabbed it as they drove past the first time. He'd taken pictures but hadn't zeroed in on that. He packed his camera in its case for the time being and slung it crosswise on his chest.

Rhodes slipped around the house and went to the back door. He knocked, but there was no answer. He pushed open the door and called out, "Hello, anyone here?"

Again, no answer. But he had seen somebody upstairs. Was that the person who had left? A few minutes later Merk joined him at the doorstep. "Any reason to go inside and check?"

The two looked at each other. They had no legal right to enter. But this was looking more than slightly suspicious. Deciding to take a chance, they went in, weapons in hand. The downstairs looked completely uninhabited. No furniture was in the living room, outside of a single chair and a footstool beside the fireplace. The kitchen cupboards were bare, and the fridge was empty. Obviously, nobody was living here.

Merk and Rhodes swept upstairs and found one room with a single bed, the other two were empty. The hall bathroom was as well. The en suite bath had a toothbrush and toothpaste, but that was it. The sinks were dry; the bathtub was too and looked as if it hadn't been used in a while.

They had no idea who was here earlier, but as he hadn't

hung around, they were short of getting answers. They ran lightly down the stairs and stopped at the door to the garage. At the count of three, they opened it and swept inside. They found no guns or other weapons.

But there were explosives—dynamite.

"Shit." Merk quickly phoned Levi while Rhodes retrieved his camera from its case. By the time they had it all cataloged, they'd been here way too long.

Levi would call the police and somehow let them know what was inside the garage.

BUOYED BY THAT success, they hopped into their vehicle and headed to the second house. This time they knew better and quickly approached to take images of the entire place, including any nearby vehicles, no matter how inoperable they looked. None were found under the carport or in the attached garage. They entered through the backyard once again and did a full sweep of the house. Nothing. Back in the truck, Rhodes called Levi. "Levi, the second house is completely empty, no sign of anyone or anything. No one has lived here for a while."

"Good to know. Head off to the third location. You're making great time. See if you can get this next one done before nightfall."

BY THE TIME they hit the third house, darkness had settled in. That was both good and bad. They needed light to search the place, and if no lights were on, it would be obvious when somebody turned them on. This two-story house was surrounded by trees on a large lot. The house was on the small rise of a hill and appeared to have a walkout-style downstairs. Neighbors were all around, but again it was a heavily treed area, so nobody could really see anyone or anything.

Merk and Rhodes parked on the shadowed shoulder of the road farther up and walked back. No vehicle was parked in the long sweeping driveway. Nobody answered their knock at the door either. The garage was unlocked, so they slipped inside and found an old car.

Frowning—because this looked much more like a broken-down antique than somebody's driving vehicle—they went out the side door and around the back. There, with the sun setting, they were running out of natural light, and none were on inside to see. If they could get in and out now, they could look around without having to turn any on. Just as they approached from the back, they heard a door bang. They froze. With a glance to each other, they carefully slipped around to the side of the house and waited. A lone man walked onto the porch and lit a cigarette.

Rhodes studied him. He was dressed all in black and wore combat boots. From the buzzed head and tattoos, he could be anything from ex-military to a white supremacist. Rhodes dismissed the military angle as the man was unshaven and looking more ragged and violent than Rhodes would have expected.

When the man finished his cigarette, he tossed the butt onto the wooden deck and walked back inside.

Another point against him. Lit cigarettes and wood were not a good combination, and he hadn't stomped on the butt and ground it out. Neither did he separate the filter from the end. Sloppy. He was leaving DNA for the police to collect.

Merk motioned from the far side of the house. Rhodes

waited, watching as Merk snuck up to the deck, came around the side and reached for something, then disappeared back the way he came.

Rhodes quickly assessed the rear of the house. Good. They could gain interior access via the windows, but still there was no sign where the smoker had gone.

They returned to their vehicle and called Levi.

"Don't go into the house," Levi warned. "We'll put a tag on that address. But given what you said, chances are he's guarding something."

Rhodes happened to agree, but that didn't mean the guy was a criminal.

He and Merk grabbed a hotel room for the night. Their motto when traveling was easy. *Get in, get out, get home.* With any luck they'd drive into the compound tomorrow night and not too late at that.

At the hotel, they quickly downloaded and sent off to Levi all the images they had collected, including the ones Rhodes had taken of the militant-looking man smoking on the back deck. Maybe with the new facial-recognition programs they might identify him. Rhodes wasn't sure if a terrorist bombing was something Levi was looking for, or Bullard for that matter, but the fact that he and Merk had found a house with a cache of explosives was bad news no matter what country they were in.

RHODES AND MERK were up and on the road well before dawn to make the trek to the next location on their list. They stopped at the fourth house early enough that the neighbors weren't up and around yet. This time they parked around the corner and entered through the back alleyway. The rear of the house had a large porch that hid them from view—of the neighbors at least. As Rhodes went to open the door, they realized it had already been broken into. Taking a picture of the busted lock and doorframe, they pushed it open and called out, "Anybody home?"

"Hello, is anyone here?"

With a glance to each other, they both pulled their weapons and moved in, one high, the other low. They swept the first floor, moving in tandem. They knew the drill. No one was prepared to take a bullet at this point in his life. The downstairs was completely empty. But somebody had broken into the house for a reason. Unless they'd come in to clean it out.

They moved upstairs and found it completely empty as well. The staircase to the attic wasn't latched. They looked at each other, and Rhodes lowered the access. Merk went up first. They stopped in the empty attic and looked around, puzzled. Something had been here. The place was spotless, no sign of dust collecting, like the cleaning service had come through, or this had all been emptied recently. At the far side of the attic were bags of some sort. The two studied them carefully before going closer.

The odor hit them first as they approached.

They found two dead men. Both wrapped in clear plastic and tied up with ropes. From the decomposition already working and the fluids filling the corners of the plastic, the dead men had been here for at least a few days if not a few weeks. Careful not to disturb them, Merk and Rhodes combed the rest of the small room. Nothing else had been left behind.

It would be damn hard identifying their faces through the plastic. Rhodes took pictures anyway and sent the images to Levi. Rhodes didn't know what the hell was going on, but it was a damn good thing somebody was checking out these houses. Back outside again, they took several deep breaths of fresh air and waited for Levi to get back to them.

"Levi?" Rhodes asked as he answered his phone. "Not exactly what we expected to find."

"Definitely not. I called the cops there. Stay at the scene. Explain that you're working for us, and you were looking to speak with the inhabitants of the house. Don't give them any details, just direct them to me. Say that you found the door ajar, broken into, and went in to investigate."

"What about the house with dynamite?"

"The police raided that house. You can watch it on the news," Levi answered in a laconic tone. "Some good media won't hurt the local police."

Rhodes laughed, but he wasn't at all impressed with having to wait for the cops or the upcoming explanations. He and Merk sat down on the back porch and did as instructed. They'd been in this situation before.

When the cops arrived, he and Merk answered what few questions there were and quickly showed the men the bodies. After that, they were escorted off the property and asked to wait for investigators to question them.

The wait was just long enough that by the time they hit the road again, it would be lucky—if not impossible—to make it home tonight. They still had one more address to check out.

"Damn," Merk said. "I told Katina I'd be home tonight for sure."

"There is no *for sure* in this business. Particularly with Levi."

"Dynamite and dead bodies? Who would have thought?"

"And what's the connection?"

THEY WERE STILL several hours away from the fifth house. Of course, this was the furthest away.

It was late afternoon when they pulled up in front of it. After what they'd found at the first and fourth houses, they had no idea what to expect here. When a family with small kids came out the door, playing in the front yard, they wondered if they had the wrong house. They double-checked the address with Levi, but sure enough a family lived here.

The three little kids all appeared to be under six years old. Mom and Dad were here, as was a puppy. It was the epitome of the happy American family.

Merk and Rhodes drove around the neighborhood, took a few pictures and headed along the back alley. This wasn't what they were expecting.

On Levi's instructions they were given the okay to head home. Damn good thing. They were more than ready to return.

Chapter 3

WITH MERK AND Rhodes both gone, Sienna found the house quiet and lonely. She and Katina naturally gravitated together. In fact, Katina came into the office to help out. She was a fast learner. And her memory was a huge help.

When Sienna got up this morning, she'd found Stone and Lissa had returned from a visit to Lissa's parents. An olive branch of some kind was being offered in exchange. Sienna didn't know the full story, but Lissa appeared to be a little happier about her parents. Then again, she had Stone at her side. And he'd make anybody happy. That man looked like a great big teddy bear and obviously adored Lissa. She was lucky.

It made Sienna sad in a way.

Here it was, fast becoming couples' land. Between Levi and Ice, Stone and Lissa—and now Merk and Katina, the last pairing that had happened while she was gone tying up her former life—she was feeling a little lost and lonely. And that was stupid. The time for that was when she'd been hitchhiking her way across the country, figuring out what her purpose in life was.

Not now that she was here with a job and a beautiful place to live with a very decent paycheck. Who knew how life would end up? She had never expected to be here, particularly finding out they were friends of Jarrod's. There was something very synchronistic about that.

In particular, seeing Rhodes.

Now that she'd handed over to Levi whatever information on the banks she had found, she returned to the basic bookkeeping and office work that in a way she loved. Although it was mundane, dull, and boring, she could blindly do it, dreaming about everything else in the world. When she heard someone at the office door, she looked up to find Katina.

"Do you realize that none of us have any hobbies?" Katina asked. "Nobody here plays music, seems to paint or draw, or do anything along those lines. I wonder why."

Sienna smiled. "Do you have any?"

Katina slumped in her chair. "No. But I plan to. I always wanted to play the guitar and learn to paint. But it's probably a good thing I don't learn the guitar for your sake's, and I doubt I would do very well painting because I really can't draw." She laughed. "I do like to garden, but have you ever seen a place lend itself less to a garden? This is a cement compound."

"True enough, but you can certainly do a lot with planters. Imagine great big cedar ones all over the place. It would really warm up the compound." She nodded toward the door. "Talk to Alfred. He seems like somebody who would love to have a garden. Particularly if it was an herb one."

Katina brightened. "That might be good for me. I never had a place where I could grow things before. I lived in a small apartment."

"And how is it working out for you and Merk here?" Sienna asked carefully. "And if it's too personal, I'm sorry."

There was silence for a minute as Katina studied Sienna's

face. "Are you asking because of Rhodes?" Her tone was light, humorous.

Sienna felt the heat wash up her neck. "Is it that obvious?"

"It has been since the two of you met. Everybody's noticed," Katina said, her grin wide. "Sparks. But it seems like very controlled ones."

Sienna gave her a look. "My brother and Rhodes are friends. That means I'm a no-no to him."

At that, Katina laughed. "Well, you just have to change his mind. You're an adult, not a little sister anymore, and Jarrod can butt right out. You get to make these choices on your own."

"Yes, except Rhodes will never see me as anything but Jarrod's little sister."

Katina leaned forward and whispered, "Take him to bed. He won't know what happened to him."

At that Sienna snickered. The idea appealed to her. Yet she didn't want to mess things up with Rhodes or her life here. Especially if her relationship with him wouldn't be a long-term scenario. That would just make working together very uncomfortable.

And that was the last thing she wanted. This was his work and his home. She was the newcomer. She didn't want to upset the apple cart just because she was attracted to him.

"I can't do that to him. He'll think it's a mistake later and hate himself."

"You worry too much. Rhodes is a big boy. Besides, once he chooses, it'd be a decision forever. His loyalty is something else. All of them together have formed a family network here that I've never seen anywhere else. It's really wonderful for them."

Katina looked out the window, seemingly someplace far off. "I had worried I wouldn't fit in. That I would be the interloper. Or that I would in some way disrupt that sense of family." She glanced over at Sienna and said, "You were even here before me. But what I found is that the family unit expanded. It's elastic. It opens and closes as it needs to. And now I feel like I belong."

"That doesn't mean there's anything between Rhodes and me."

"Of course it doesn't. But if you don't work toward that, there never will be." With a cheerful smile, Katina stood up and said, "I'll head down and see if Alfred needs any help in the kitchen." She glanced around the room and added, "You don't need me, do you?"

Sienna shook her head. "No, I'm almost done with the paperwork. The guys should be back soon anyway. Apparently, they had quite the trip."

"That's true. They found dead bodies." Katina shuddered. "Kitchen and office work is much better suited for me." She gave Sienna a beaming smile and left.

Sienna watched her walk away. Katina was just so cheerful and upbeat. She was fun to be around. Sienna hadn't considered herself gloomy, but she'd definitely lost a lot of her bounce when her former job fell apart.

The phone rang. Bullard again. "Hello, Bullard. Now what?"

He laughed. "Do you think I only call you when I need some help?"

"Of course you do." She looked around the empty room, tilted her chair back, kicking her feet up on the desk. "It is what I expect."

"Not everybody in the world is out to use you," he said

in a cheerful tone. "Lots of good people are in the world too."

"Those good people would use me too," she said drily. "Back to business. What do you need?"

He laughed. "Nothing. I wanted to give you an update. The first bank found their employee—the older guy I was telling you about, the IT manager, who will be retiring soon. He started pilfering off the top. He confessed readily. Trying to save his son, who could be involved in something much darker as he's the one who had the spreadsheets."

"Were they working together?"

"Not according to the father. His son is completely innocent if you listened to him."

"I doubt it." She laughed. "But the father almost got away with it." She stared at her desk. "I caught some account numbers on the code you sent. The transactions were all international."

"That makes sense. I'll let you know when any of the other banks get back to me." His tone turned calm. "I owe you one." And he hung up.

She was still smiling when Levi walked into the room. He raised an eyebrow and asked, "What's up?"

She quickly brought him up to date on Bullard's case.

"This is really good work, Sienna."

"I didn't do anything. It was easy stuff." She shrugged self-consciously. "That part was just luck."

He laughed. "Something's only easy because you're good at it." He headed to his desk.

She studied him as he sat down again and asked in a low voice she hoped was calm and disinterested, "When are the guys getting back?"

"They're on their way now."

She nodded. "Right. Going to be late then." She looked over at him and asked, "Do you have any other work for me right now?"

"No, you've done a ton already this week. It's much appreciated."

She shut off her computer and stood up, saying, "In that case, I'll see if I can round up a cup of coffee."

She wandered out of the room and headed toward the kitchen. The compound was huge, and a dozen or so people lived here. There wasn't a whole lot of social activity in this remote area, but when she had a chance, she did take trips into town. She didn't want to feel like she was forced to stay in the compound. Because she wasn't. She had gone with Katina, and sometimes Ice, to watch a movie or two in town, plus lunch outings and shopping. Sometimes the guys joined them. But her needs were minimal, and it was senseless to pay for a meal when Alfred was such a good cook.

In truth, she was bored. And she hadn't expected that. Although she'd settled in here, with her brother leaving, there was a sense of loss. It was compounded by the fact Rhodes was gone these last few days. Then again, he didn't really see her when he was here.

She wandered through the kitchen now with a cup of coffee in hand and headed out to the garage. She didn't know very much about electronics. Harrison was bent over a laptop, swearing. She stepped up beside him and said, "What's going on that has you so upset?"

He looked up at her with surprise and then grinned. "I'm not upset. This is actually fun for me. I like to see what people have hidden on their laptops and what they were doing with secret files they thought were erased. People always presume that, if they delete something on their computer, or damage the hard drive, it's gone." He shook his head. "And it isn't."

She nodded. "Same thing with code." She frowned, looked at the mess, and asked, "Is there anything I can do to help?"

He looked over at her and said, "If you're serious, yes. Try to sort through all the different cables and set up bins for each type. Sometimes I have to hook up multiple units together, and if we don't have an orderly system, it can take time to find what I need."

She walked over to what appeared to be a brand-new storage system and asked, "Do you need things in any particular order?"

"If you use those bins, we can move them around to suit us."

Taking a closer look, she realized the plastic boxes detached, so as long as she stuck one thing in each, he could organize them as he wanted. She turned her attention back to the large workbench completely covered with cables.

She sorted through what she could in the stash and put the obviously distinct ones into the top three empty bins and then separated the remaining pile. She found everything from standard-issue cables to printer cables to a bunch of cut wires and big long ribbons of cloth-looking cables, plus a rat's nest of who-knew-what. These were hubs, but she had no idea if they were to come apart or not. She set them off to one side to ask questions later and quickly delved into the big snake pile on top.

She knew software. This venture into hardware was different.

When the big double doors opened behind her, she turned in surprise. Sure enough it was Rhodes and Merk, driving the small truck. They pulled up, parked, and she just barely caught sight of Katina as she raced around to dive into Merk's arms. As he held Katina tight, Sienna's gaze bounced to Rhodes and off again. It was enough to see him studying her.

She quickly turned back and nudged Harrison to let him know the guys were here. And then she said, "I didn't know what to do with the rest of the stuff." She pointed out the items still on the desk. "I did get the others in the bins."

"Wow, this looks great," he said with a big smile. "What a huge help." He glanced at the desk and said, "Okay, these guys we can do this with." He quickly separated off the rest of the electronics, and as she watched, he tossed things into different bins.

She could have done that but not without knowing what he wanted. When she turned around, Rhodes was still glaring at her. She glared right back. "What the hell's wrong with you?" she snapped.

"You," he roared.

She fisted her hands on her hips and studied him. "Now what?"

"You've already put in a full day. What the hell are you doing out here helping Harrison?"

"Whatever I'm doing is my business," she snapped. She glanced over at Harrison, but he had wisely stepped out of the way and was busy washing up.

She caught sight of Katina and Merk, both hiding their grins as they walked toward the door. Katina called back, "Rhodes, we held dinner for you, so it's time to wash up and come in."

As they disappeared, Harrison went in right after them, leaving her and Rhodes alone in the garage.

"Look at you, covered in dirt."

She glanced down and smiled. "But it's honest dirt. And it will wash off. Just like I will. It's just jeans and a T-shirt. I can get changed easily enough." She tried to brush off her clothes, but it was pretty ineffectual. She shrugged. "And it doesn't matter. Dinners waiting, so let's go."

Rhodes stepped toward the main door, then turned and said, "Does that mean you haven't eaten yet either?"

She glanced down at her watch to see it was seven o'clock. "No, I haven't. I guess I have been out here for a few hours with Harrison."

"So, as soon as your brother disappears, you stop taking care of yourself?" he asked.

She gasped. "That's so unfair." She fisted her hands on her hips again—which seemed to be the stance she preferred all too often when facing him—and said, "It doesn't matter if he's here or not." She hopped onto the step in front of him so she could meet his glare head-on and said, "Just because my brother is gone doesn't mean I need another man to step up and take his role." She turned her back on Rhodes and stormed inside.

She headed into the kitchen to wash up. When she went to the long dining table, the only open space was near Rhodes. Like hell she wanted to sit next to him. But everybody was already in place, so she took the empty spot without being rude or causing a scene, which would draw even more attention to her and Rhodes. She sat down beside him and completely ignored him for the rest of the meal.

HE HADN'T MEANT to snap at her. But they'd driven like crazy to get home when they had. And he'd been looking forward to seeing her the whole way. Only to find her with Harrison. But seeing her work herself to the bone drove him crazy. He should've realized she needed other interests and had likely been curious about what went on here.

Besides, Harrison would've accepted any help coming his way. When he got into a project that had anything to do with electronics, they lost him for hours. That was both good and bad. But Rhodes couldn't stop wondering if something was going on between Harrison and Sienna. He gripped his fork a little too tightly and stabbed the chunk of roast beef a little too hard. *Ease back, buddy. Ease back.* Rhodes also really liked that she stood up to him.

Still, he was coming on a bit strong. She was right. She had older brothers, and she didn't need Rhodes watching over her too. At least not in that role. But the only one left to him was as a friend, and he didn't want that. He wanted so much more.

He deliberately avoided looking at all the couples at the table. It was increasingly obvious that Levi and Ice's company had too much in common with Mason's group. And they'd all be angry if he said something about it, but…it was pretty hard not to think about it.

Because he was one of the men without a partner.

Sighing, he finished off his plate and pushed it back. "Thanks, Alfred. As usual that was fantastic."

Other voices joined in with their appreciation. Rhodes slipped off the bench, grabbed his plate and carried it into the kitchen. He rinsed it and loaded it in the dishwasher himself, grabbed a cup of coffee, stuck his head into the room where he had been sitting and said, "I'm done for the night. See you in the morning." And he turned and walked to his suite.

It was early, but that wasn't the point. He just needed time alone, away from the others. In his suite, he quickly unpacked, had a shower and set up his laptop. He had research to do to see how much the news had come up with on the nameless bodies he and Merk had found. Two dead men had put a huge damper on the trip, because no matter what one thought about criminals, they had been a father, brother, husband, and/or son to somebody. And people somewhere would be in pain right now for the loss of those men.

There was also no proof they were the bad guys either. For all Rhodes knew, they were innocent.

Very strange indeed. Unless the house was being used for drugs versus dynamite, and something went wrong. Maybe the thieves had a falling out, and those two men were left behind. They could be brothers who own the house and were taken out as a point of convenience.

Sometimes life just sucked.

He quickly checked the news media, pulling up the local newspapers, but found no mention of either man.

This was an odd case. They weren't seeing the whole picture, and he didn't like that. He wanted to know more, do more. He wanted closure, and how the hell would they get that when it wasn't their case?

At a knock on the door, he stood up and opened it to find Levi.

He leaned against the doorframe and said, "We got two identifications on the men found."

Rhodes straightened. "And?"

"They were cousins. Both with ties to the drug trade. Neither seemed to have any connection to the house or to Bullard's bank fraud case."

"Odd that they would've been found there then."
Rhodes frowned. "Obviously, there is a connection as he
gave us the addresses."

"Not if there was infighting among the thieves, and these
two lost the argument."

"Anything's possible." Rhodes added, "What about the
raid on the house with the dynamite?"

"The police tracked down the owners, currently living
on the West Coast. It was a rental unit. They have no idea
what was going on there, and they don't have any answers."

"That wouldn't have been a pleasant surprise for them to
hear either. So, no answers there." He studied Levi and said,
"I don't like only getting bits and pieces about this job. We
got a house with explosives, a different residential address a
long way away that probably housed drugs but had two dead
men. What's the connection? Is this our job, yours, or
Bullard's? And how does any of this pertain to the code that
Sienna was looking at?" He threw up his hands in frustration. "At least in a normal job that's fully ours, we have all
the information. We have the targets. We know what's going
down. In this case, it feels like we're subcontracting to
Bullard."

"And we are. It's new. It's different—and maybe it's not
something we want to do a lot of—but we are closer to the
Dallas bank than Bullard. We're the locals here. The same
holds true vice versa. At any future point in time, when we
need some information that he can access easier than we can
from here, then we'll subcontract to him."

"I understand that in theory. It just feels … odd. Make
that wrong." He gave a Levi lopsided grin. "You know how I
like to have a target."

Levi laughed. "Sure you do. Maybe you should go to the

fitness room and work out some of that frustration."

"That's not a bad idea actually. My own research on the men to see if the media had picked up a trail didn't find very much on anything."

"Several jurisdictions I know of were working on this. But nobody has any information to help."

"What were the names of the cousins?"

"Martin and Jeremy Lewis." Levi smacked the wall and said, "I'll be in the office for the next hour if you want to talk." And he turned and walked away.

Rhodes wasn't sure what the last line meant, but figured it was probably an open-ended comment. Still, Levi's suggestion about a workout was a good idea.

They'd put in a large fitness area soon after they got here. He quickly changed into a muscle shirt and shorts, grabbed a towel and water bottle, then headed to the lower floor. The fitness room was across from the medical center. Thankfully, *that* area was clean and empty. They'd christened that room already many times over.

He walked in, dropped his towel, and headed for the free weights. He did his upper body exercises for a good ten minutes, then had the feeling he wasn't alone. When he turned, of course, it was Sienna.

She was doing floor exercises, completely ignoring him.

Well, he could do the same. He quickly did another set, put his weights down, stretched out his muscles and caught sight of her in the mirrors. She was now doing push-ups. And man, could she move. He prided himself on a perfect push-up, but when it came to a woman's form, she was knocking it to the floor. He wanted to stand here and admire her, but that wouldn't do his own workout any good. Besides, she was damn prickly, and he was pretty sure she didn't like anybody watching her.

He returned to his upper body weights. By the time he focused on her again, she'd left. It had been a perfect opportunity to apologize, and he hadn't taken it. That was the problem with apologies. They really needed to happen on the spot, before it spun into bigger arguments over nothing. Now he was frustrated again.

He walked to the floor area, dropped to the mat and did fifty push-ups. Then he added another twenty-five, just a single left-hand version and then twenty-five more on his right. Still needing more, he flipped onto his back and did one hundred crunches.

By the time he was done, he felt a little on the mellower side again. As he stood and walked back out, towel slung around his neck, he caught sight of Sienna in the medical clinic. She was wandering through the room, studying everything. He watched her for a long minute before stepping through the doorway. "Do you have any medical training?"

She shot him a look, then shook her head. "It's really not my thing." She waved her arms at the clean cabinets. "It's like some kind of big mystery happens here. I'm fascinated and repelled at the same time."

He grinned. "I don't think you're alone in that."

As she walked toward him, as if intending to step past him to head to her suite, he said abruptly, "I'm sorry."

She turned and looked at him. "What for?"

Uncomfortable already, he bristled. "For acting like your older brother."

"Well, that's one brotherly thing you didn't get right. Jarrod would never apologize." She grinned. "However, apology accepted. Just don't do it again."

He rolled his eyes. "You don't make it easy."

"And I don't intend to either." She walked away, then turned and continued walking backward as she asked him, "Any news on the men you found?"

"Cousins. Last name Lewis, first names Martin and Jeremy. Both with connections to the drug trade."

She froze. Her gaze widened. "Those were two names I connected accounts to." She frowned. "I forgot to give that to Bullard."

"What?" He took several steps toward her.

She spun around and raced to the stairs, calling back, "I have to talk to Levi." Then she was gone from sight.

Like hell she would keep him in the dark. He picked up the pace and raced up the stairs behind her.

Chapter 4

"**L**EVI?" SHE STOOD hesitantly at the office door. Both Ice and Levi had their heads bent over blueprints of some kind. She knew they had plans for an expansion to the compound but didn't know what that entailed exactly.

Levi looked up and smiled. "What's up, Sienna?"

She ventured inside a few steps and said, "Rhodes just told me about the cousins found dead in the house. I'm pretty sure those were the two names I deciphered from the code and spreadsheets Bullard sent."

Levi's gaze widened. "I wondered why they sounded familiar. I couldn't find anything that would give me a reason to confirm that though." He stood up straight, walked to the table where she had placed the codes with her scratch pad of decoded names. He tapped the second line and said, "You're right. J. Lewis, M. Lewis. Also, the initials R.F."

"And those names had the lower figures by them," Sienna said. "It's potentially a smaller deal. Of course, this is just supposition until we get more answers."

"But we can also track a lot of information about those cousins now ourselves," Ice said.

She walked to a desk in the far corner. Sienna recognized it as the one she usually used, but as they all shifted, depending on who was here and who was gone, she didn't know if anybody had a dedicated computer.

Ice sat down, opened the laptop and said, "I'm not as good as some of the guys, but I'm learning."

Levi grinned. "We don't do anything illegal," he explained to Sienna, "but we do have access to a lot of databases, including police files. And if we can't get enough information on our own, we have friends in places who can."

"No arrests on either name," Ice said. "But we have sealed juvie files for both."

"I'm not surprised. We won't get those unsealed."

"Don't need to," Ice said simply. "The fact that they even exist means their teenage years were something of a life of crime."

"Any other members of the family?" Levi asked.

Sienna waited, wishing she could be more involved. Then realized she had access to some of that information as well. She went to her laptop and turned it on. Within minutes she said, "Martin has a brother. Both parents are still alive. Jeremy has a sister, and his mother is alive. The cousins were raised next door to each other."

She studied the addresses in front of her. "The families actually own their houses. Maybe they had money or came into some. There are no mortgages on either."

"So both men were raised with lots of family, good values, and obviously not a poor living area if the parents owned their houses," Ice theorized.

"I can't confirm that about the neighborhood," Sienna said, "but it wouldn't be too hard to double-check. Not that it helps much."

"There's often no reason why some kids go south like that," Ice said. "Also, maybe they just went into that world to make money, and that's how the parents paid off their houses." She looked at Levi. "About time to bring in a few of our connections, pass over some of this information and see what they might have to offer."

"Or call Bullard first," Sienna said. Both turned to look at her as she smiled. "Or not." She raised her hands and shrugged. "Don't quite know how all this works. But normally we would get as much information on our side before offering any to somebody else."

Ice laughed. "I like the way you think."

Levi checked his watch and said, "Perfect. It's about six in the morning over there. I'll call Bullard now." He pulled out his phone, turned to look at Ice and said, "I'll let you talk to him."

In a surprise move she reached up and kissed Levi on the cheek. "You can talk to him, sweetie." She walked from the room. "It's getting late. I'm headed to our suite."

Sienna shut down her laptop as she heard Levi talking to Bullard and with a small wave, turned and walked toward the office door. And that's when she saw Rhodes, leaning against the doorway, arms crossed. She glared at him. "Did you hear the whole thing?"

He raised his eyebrows at her tone and said, "Sure. Why not? I didn't interrupt or have anything to add."

His words were correct, and his voice was level, but the glint in his eye made her suspicious.

She brushed past him. "Levi's talking to Bullard now. So, if you want to talk to him about this, you'll have to wait."

"Are you heading to bed now?"

An odd tone was in his voice. She turned to look at him. "I'm going to take a shower."

"Ah."

She stopped, pivoted to face him fully and glared at him. "What does that mean?"

He raised his eyebrows once again.

She shook her head. "Don't raise your eyebrows like that. What do you mean?"

"Nothing. I should take a shower too." He whistled as he walked past her and tossed back, "Too bad we can't have one together and conserve water."

And then, just like that, he was gone. She made her way into her suite and slammed the door, locking it behind her. She leaned against it. Then slowly sank to the floor.

Because now the only thought in her head was of the two of them, making passionate love, bodies twisting in hot water, completely into each other.

Damn him. Now she needed a cold shower.

THAT WAS MEAN of him. Yet he grinned. *Too bad.* She was just way-too-damn distracting. He should have spoken to Jarrod when he was here before he went off on another mission.

Jarrod had to know his sister hooking up with someone here was a possibility. There were several single men. Attraction happened. And way too fast in some cases. He headed to his suite and stripped to get into the shower. He laughed again at his comment and the look of shock on her face. He stepped into the water, then realized though he had said it as a joke, his body was already thinking about the two of them in the damn water. And his body wasn't taking no for an answer.

He was forced to turn down the temperature to cool himself off in order to get through it. By the time he wrapped himself in a towel, dried off and stepped into the bedroom, he was pissed at himself. By teasing her, he was teasing himself, and that was the last thing he needed. He glanced at the time and realized it was still pretty early. He put on his sweats and a T-shirt and headed downstairs to watch a movie. The living room was empty, and that was the way he liked it. He turned on the monster seventy-two-inch TV. The one thing they all agreed on when they decided they needed a TV was that they would buy the biggest and most badass one they could find.

He grinned as he checked through the movie listings until he found a hard-core action flick. Before pressing Play, he walked to the kitchen to grab some popcorn. He put the bag in the microwave, poured a shot of whiskey and when the microwave finished, carried the drink and popcorn back into the living room and stopped. He was no longer alone.

Sienna had the remote, checking out a chick flick on the screen.

"Ah, hell, no," he said. He put down the popcorn and his drink and said, "No chick flicks allowed in the house."

She turned, one eyebrow raised, and said, "As a man you're afraid of romance. Or maybe it's sex."

He glared at her. He remembered all the comments he'd made way back when about her temper. Obviously, he had pricked it well tonight. He decided to change his tactic. He bent in front of her and kissed her. "Anytime you want somebody to warm your bed, you just have to say so," he said. He snatched the remote from her hand and immediately flicked it back to the movie he had set up.

"Besides killing, is there anything else you guys like to do?"

He hit Play, and the movie started immediately. He

zoomed into a big action scene where a building was being blown up. He grinned. "Love this stuff."

She snorted. "Of course you do. No plot, nor character, just blow shit up."

But she didn't leave. She curled up in the opposite corner of the couch and watched it with him. About ten minutes later he realized she had grabbed the entire bowl of popcorn and held it close to her chest, on the side away from him. He looked at her in outrage. "First you to try to steal my movie, then my popcorn."

She glanced at him innocently and said, "While I eat this popcorn, why don't you get yourself another one?"

He glared at her and chuckled. "I have a better idea." He got up and moved right beside her, touching her from hip to knee, wrapped an arm around her and said, "We'll share."

She tried to wiggle free, but that wasn't happening.

Finally, she subsided and glared at him.

"That'll teach you to take over a man's domain without his permission."

"Like it's yours." She scoffed. "Do you think I don't know how to handle you guys? Remember, Jarrod's only one of four brothers I have. And they are all big, tough, macho guys like you. You're nothing special."

He had meant to reach into the popcorn bowl but her smaller hand slipped in under his, and she snagged up the last of it, popping the bunch in her mouth. Then she glared at him, like a challenge.

He stared at the empty bowl and then glared at her in mock outrage. The trouble was, he didn't want to move, not at all. He thought about getting another bowl to share, then realized as soon as he moved, she would leave. He'd much rather stay here.

"Think you're so smart, do you?" She turned her head away, kicked her legs up between them and sat curled up in the corner. "I'm not getting browbeaten by male bullying."

"I didn't bully you," he said. But he settled back slightly, giving her space. He looked down woefully at the bowl still in her arms. "You're the bully. You ate all the popcorn."

She glanced at the bowl, then laughed. "Okay, maybe I am. But I was hungry."

"Didn't you get enough to eat at dinnertime?" He picked up his whiskey and settled back. "There is also some alcohol around, if you want a drink."

She looked at the glass with vague interest. "I'm not much of a hard drinker. A glass of wine now and then, that's a different story."

"I can get you one if you'd like. We have both red and white."

She hesitated, then shook her head. "No, I shouldn't."

"Why shouldn't you?" he asked with interest. "It's safe here. Even if you drank too much, nobody would take advantage of you. I might have to put you in your bed because you can't get there on your own, but somebody would see the job done."

She snorted. "How you would love a chance to do that." She shook her head. "Nope, my ex-boyfriend was a heavy drinker. Still not terribly comfortable around them."

"Having a drink in the evening is not being a drinker." But he shrugged and settled deeper into the cushion. In his head, he wondered just how bad of a heavy drinker the guy had been. Had he beaten her? Rhodes glanced over at her, but she hadn't shown any fear when he had pushed her boundaries. And that was a good thing.

Besides, if Jarrod had any idea that the ex might have

knocked her around, he'd have taken care of the guy immediately.

Rhodes settled back to watch the movie, happy she had stayed with him. She moaned after a couple action scenes and groaned at a couple dumb one-liners, but hey, he didn't put this movie on because he was concerned about the eloquent conversation between the characters. It was exactly what he needed to escape. And the longer they sat here, the more she relaxed. Eventually her legs stretched out beside him, not quite touching, not avoiding him either. But she was totally at ease, and that's what he wanted.

At one point, she pulled her feet up and accidentally touched him. "Sorry," she muttered.

"Doesn't matter. The couch is huge."

At that, she stretched out her legs. There wasn't quite enough room, so he picked her feet up and put them on his lap. "Just leave them here. You'll be more comfortable."

At that she tucked a pillow under her head and turned her attention back to the movie.

By the time the credits rolled through, he was grinning like a fool. He always liked those movies. A large group of men going after the bad guys, along the way rescuing the damsel in distress. Just like his life. He shut off the TV and turned to ask, "What did you think of it?"

And stopped. She'd fallen asleep. He shook his head. He didn't even know when she'd nodded off.

He got up, took his empty glass and bowl into the kitchen, rinsed and loaded both in the dishwasher, and came back out, wondering what he should do with her.

He checked his watch. It was 10:30 p.m. Definitely time for her to go to bed. He reached out a gentle hand and tried to shake her awake. She body-rolled with his movements but never woke up. He frowned and gave her a harder shake. She mumbled, tried to turn over, but the couch wasn't giving her any room. Finally, in frustration, she fell back asleep.

He didn't think he'd seen anybody sleep quite that way. But he had an easy answer. He reached under her body, picked her up in his arms and quietly walked to the elevator, hit the button and stepped inside. He could feel his muscles work as he had lifted her, but thankfully everything seemed to be going just fine. His original injuries caused him some concern, but this last year with heavy training, he was back into his prime condition again.

On the second floor, he walked to her suite and had to shuffle her in his arms to get her door open.

Thankfully, she'd left it unlocked. He nudged it wider with his foot, and walked carefully over to the bed. Then he frowned because of course, it was made. He pulled back the covers and sheets and laid her down. He quickly took off her shoes and stopped, staring at her shirt and jeans. If he undressed her, she'd be pissed. But how could she get a good rest if he didn't?

He decided to go for it, taking off her jeans and T-shirt. Tucking her under the covers, he folded her clothes nicely, leaving them on the other side of the bed. At the door, he turned off the light, glanced over at the sleeping beauty and whispered, "Good night."

She didn't respond. Just snuggled deeper into the covers. He shook his head at her ability to sleep so deeply, so fast. He'd had high hopes for sleep himself. Now he wasn't so sure. Instead of pictures of great action scenes dancing in his head, he would see a model-perfect body twisting beneath him.

By the time he made it to his suite, he contemplated another cold shower.

Chapter 5

WHEN SIENNA WOKE up the next morning, she twisted uncomfortably, wondering what was pulling at her ribs. She rolled onto her back and realized she was still wearing her bra. She struggled to remember last night, anything past the movie and sitting on the couch with Rhodes. She threw back the covers and, relieved to see she still wore panties, headed to the bathroom, took a quick shower, dressed in fresh clothing and headed out. She snagged her cell phone as she left, checking the time. It was only 7:30.

She wouldn't be the first downstairs. She wasn't sure Alfred ever slept, as he had to get up at some godforsaken hour to bake those always fresh cinnamon buns and other goodies he offered them.

Sure enough he was there, as were most of the men. "Don't any of you guys sleep?" she asked in a half mumble. She headed for the coffeepot and poured herself a large mug. Turning around, she sat down at the table. She'd had lots of sleep, but her body said it wasn't done yet.

"What's on tap for today, Levi?" Rhodes asked.

"How does Sienna feel about discussing some of this with the DA's office in Dallas?"

She stared at Levi. "Me?" she squeaked. "Why should I go?"

"Because you can explain the codes and names you found."

"Wouldn't it be easier to do that on the phone?" She'd never done any fieldwork. Even with her old job.

"Possibly. But Rhodes needs to check out a couple more places."

Her heart sank. At the same time, her nerve endings came alive. She was going with Rhodes? That would not be a good thing. Especially if that meant a night at a hotel. She dropped her gaze to her coffee mug and lifted it to take a sip. In her mind, she thought it was foolish. "How many hours are we talking?"

"If we leave now, we might get back tonight," Rhodes said quietly. "Otherwise, we'd have to stay overnight. It also depends on what kind of trouble we run into."

Immediately she shook her head. "Remember, I don't do trouble."

Everybody at the table laughed.

"Easy for you to say," Rhodes quipped, "considering you came here through trouble. But when it happens, nobody's ever prepared for it."

She really didn't want to, but she wasn't sure how to come up with an excuse not to. She also didn't understand what the point was.

Ice walked in then, sitting down at the table. She looked over at Sienna. "Did Levi ask you?"

"If you mean about seeing the DA, yes, he did. But it doesn't make any sense to me."

"Don't know if you heard that they found more pages of code, but they don't really understand what they're looking at. There has to be a reason these sections were printed off. This time there are names."

Sienna immediately shook her head. "They will have a whole team of specialists more capable of sorting through that paperwork than I am."

Levi nodded. "Maybe we should say they don't have anybody they trust. They're afraid some of those names on that list are coming out of their offices and higher up."

"Oh." Her shoulders slumped. That she did understand. It made sense then. Betrayal happened at all levels. And often those were the hardest to prove, the higher-ups. And they often had to bring in somebody from an outside firm to handle it.

She considered the risks, realized that Rhodes would be there with her, something she desperately wanted, even if it was really bad for her, and nodded. "Okay, let's hope we can be back tonight."

Ice immediately shook her head. "That won't happen. They have meetings set up for you today and tomorrow."

Sienna raised her gaze to study Ice's expression but found only sincerity in hers. "Remember, you guys, I haven't had any field experience. This could be a really bad deal for Rhodes."

They all snorted. "Rhodes says he's up for it."

She glanced at Rhodes to see him studying her intently. She didn't know what was going on in the back of his mind, but she knew something was—a challenge and something a whole lot warmer. And she'd never backed down from one of those yet.

"Then I guess I'll pack an overnight bag."

Alfred walked in carrying a large platter of food. "You can pack a bag after breakfast. The food is hot and fresh. Eat first." He placed the food down in front of her.

Within seconds they were all eating.

Only it was a little hard to get her food down. Suddenly she was uneasy. Her tummy queasy. She only ate a little bit, but of course Alfred noticed.

"I'll pack you some food to-go." He bustled away to the kitchen.

"I don't mean to be a problem," she murmured.

Merk laughed at that. "He loves to mother us. So, let him. He sent a huge basketful of food with Rhodes and me the last time we took off."

She stood up and filled her coffee cup. "I'll be back in ten."

She headed to her suite. It was the first chance she'd had to relax after becoming the center of attention down there. She didn't know what was going on in Rhodes's mind, but she was afraid of what that meant. Because, if it was what she thought it was, she wanted that too. Was it so wrong? No, but she wasn't ready for another relationship, and if it went wrong, she'd screw up her perfect job here. Not to mention she'd have to find a new place to live. No, it was too early to risk this. She liked it here and didn't want anything to mess that up.

In her suite, she pulled out her bag and quickly packed a few pieces of clothing. As she stared at her worldly possessions, she realized even though she'd been here for close to a month, she hadn't increased her material possessions at all. She didn't have any more clothes. She had the same few pairs of jeans and underwear, and she hadn't done laundry either. Now she didn't have time to do that. There was no sense fussing. What she had would have to be enough.

Resolute, she turned, checked out her suite and felt an odd sense of good-bye. Although she'd left the compound before to come back again, there was a sense of detachment this time. And she didn't like it. She'd found a home here—she'd made herself a place. She wanted to keep it. But times were changing, obviously.

She turned out the light at the bedroom door and headed downstairs, running into Ice in the garage. "I don't have a ton of clothes to take with me," she confessed. "Even when I was gone, I hadn't bothered shopping for more. That sense of only having what I can carry still applied back then, and I can't seem to shake it even now."

Ice patted her shoulder. "Dallas has lots of malls. It's a shopping mecca. You can run into a store to collect what you need."

"That's fine as long as jeans are okay," Sienna said. "If you're expecting me to wear some kind of professional outfit for this deal, we have to shop first."

Rhodes walked into the kitchen, wearing jeans and a shirt the same color as hers too.

She smiled. "Okay, so maybe we're a matched set."

"Absolutely," he said, picking up her bag, then motioning toward the truck. "We're taking the same small pickup as last time." He tossed her bag behind the seat, turned to accept a basket of goodies from Alfred and said, "Come on. Let's go."

"No, I need coffee first," she said. "Let me grab a travel mug." As she headed toward the coffeepot, she found Alfred had two big cups and a thermos there waiting. She turned to find him right behind her. She threw her arms around his neck and gave him a big hug and kissed his cheek. "Thank you, Alfred. You're the best." She grabbed the coffee and ran.

RHODES WAITED FOR her to get in and place the coffee

mugs in the cup holders. When she didn't reach for her seat belt immediately, he said, "Buckle up."

She shot him a look but did as told.

When they were finally out of the compound, heading toward the main road, he turned to look at her. "Are you sure you're okay with this?"

She huffed beside him.

He didn't know any other word to describe it. It was like a half-snort, half-sniff, and it made him smile. "I'll take that as a yes."

Nothing but silence was her response. He shrugged. *Whatever.* They had a long way to go. It would be easier if they got along during this trip, but if not, well, he was a pro. He could handle it regardless.

After a few minutes, she turned to look at him. "Did you set this up?"

He turned in astonishment. "Hell, no."

In a small voice she said, "Oh."

"I have better things to do with my time than take cold showers in the evening," he said simply. He laughed at that. He could feel her shocked stare, but he wouldn't elaborate. Not after their conversation last night.

He drove steadily for several hours. When they came to a gas station, he pulled in and filled the tank. She hopped out and cleaned the windshield wipers, surprising him.

When he was done, she walked over to him. "Want me to drive for a bit?"

"No, I'm good. If you want more coffee or something, you can get whatever inside."

She shook her head. "No, Alfred sent lots of coffee. I do need the washroom now. Who knows when we'll be taking another break."

He paid for the gas, took the receipt, pocketed it and hopped into the truck to wait for her. He reached across and opened the basket, grabbing a handful of sandwiches from Alfred. She was right. When would they stop again? While he waited, he devoured one sandwich and was busy working on the second when she returned.

She took one look, raised her eyebrows and said, "Are you leaving me any?"

He motioned at the basket. "Help yourself."

They both ate while he returned to the road and kept going. He checked his watch. "We should be at the Dallas city limits in another twenty minutes."

"Fine. I still don't understand why I had to come."

"Sure you do." He glanced at her. "Besides Levi's probably checking out how you handle yourself. Are you afraid of getting involved in something like you were before, or are you really against fieldwork?"

She thought about the question for a long moment. "I don't know what it is. I guess I thought I'd closed that door and walked away from it. I hadn't really expected to open it again, not in these circumstances."

"Fair enough." He put on his signal, changed lanes and pulled over to the exit ramp. "We don't come across this kind of problem very often."

"If it's tracking money, it'll be in every case."

"True. Levi often handles that, and Harrison is a whiz on computers, as are you. I do a lot of that kind of work too. But none of us have the same level of skill you do. Maybe if you could teach us, we wouldn't need you to do it at all."

"Coding isn't something you just pick up," she said quietly. "Not at this level. Besides I don't know many languages. I specialized in banking software. That's it."

She seemed to brighten up after that. He had to wonder if she'd told him everything that had gone on. Did anybody really know the whole story? Or did she keep some of the darker stuff to herself? It took him back to that whole ex-boyfriend-who-had-been-a-drinker thing. He hadn't questioned the scenario originally. But now that he watched her reaction to it all, he was starting to wonder.

But he kept his concerns to himself.

He pulled out the address for where they were going and punched it into the GPS. He could've done this a long time ago, but now that they were heading into town, he'd get a better reading. He followed the instructions to the DA's office and pulled in the adjacent parking lot. He shut off the engine and turned to look at her. "Are you ready?"

"As ready as I'll ever be." And with that she opened the truck door and stepped out.

Chapter 6

S HE TOOK A deep breath and followed Rhodes into the big government-looking building. For some reason, she expected the DA to have an office in a much smaller, more private setting. She didn't know if this was normal or just set up for today. Rhodes seemed to know where he was at least.

At the DA's office, they were seated in a small boardroom at a table, waiting for the meeting to start. A few minutes later, a tall, very lean-looking male walked in. He seemed in his late fifties, with an air of cool competence as he joined them. He shook their hands and introduced himself. "I'm District Attorney Robert Forrest." He nodded as a second man joined them. "This is Bobby. He'll help you with whatever you need. He'll get the box we have collected."

Even though the two names were similiar—one was just a shortened version of the other—she worried she'd mix them up, her nervousness getting the better of her. Even gaining strength from Rhodes's presence wasn't helping much.

Robert immediately got down to business. He pulled out the sheets forwarded to him. She recognized her handwriting on one.

"Now I understand you guys know of these two men." Robert pointed to the mug shots of the cousins.

Rhodes nodded. "Yes, that's them."

"Good. And you?" He turned to look at Sienna. "You're the one who pulled the names from this series of spreadsheets, is that correct?"

"Following the pattern I saw in the software code, the banks stopped the employee who'd hacked their system. These sheets were found in his possession," she said. "Those are the names the code decoded down to."

She was very careful to say she hadn't been the one to do anything. But at the same time, Robert didn't seem interested in placing blame or giving credit.

Again, he nodded. He opened his briefcase and pulled out several more spreadsheets. "Having seen this work before, potentially you could find more information in these?"

She pulled them toward her and looked at the first one. She quickly scanned the seven sheets. "They look to be similar, yes."

"Do you see any other names?"

She frowned. "Potentially. If they decode down the same way as the other sheets, then yes, that's easy to do." She wanted to say it would be easy to have them done without her being here, but she didn't. She glanced over at his briefcase and asked, "Is there a scratch pad and pen I could use?"

Instantly both appeared in front of her. She picked up the pen, grabbed the first spreadsheet and very quickly had the first ten lines listed. She went back to the spreadsheet, noting the repetitions within the lines. On the fourth page, she came to a new name. She wrote that down, and her system continued, and soon she had them all down on the sheet of paper in front of her. She turned the pad around, pointing it to Robert so he could read the names.

He stared, and some of the color washed out of his face.

She glanced at Rhodes. Had he noticed how nervous she was? She hoped not. Once again, she didn't have an explanation for her feelings. He reached across and grabbed her fingers and squeezed them reassuringly. She relaxed some and asked, "Is that what you were expecting?"

The DA sat down in the chair heavily. "No. It's worse than that. Some of these names are pretty high up in the city."

"But there's no proof they've done anything. That's the problem," she said quietly. "Without tracking these accounts and the banks that have been hacked, there's no way to see just where they lead and what's been done under these people's names. For all we know, their identities have been stolen, and they aren't involved at all."

Robert looked at Rhodes and said, "I spoke with Levi about this. I believe your other man, Bullard, is involved on the banking end. This case is obviously global. My concern is less about the hacking and more about drugs and arms dealings in my city. But we'll obviously look in to all of it."

The door opened, and Bobby walked in, carrying a file box. He placed it beside the DA and took a seat at the back without saying a word.

The break was good timing as far as she was concerned, considering the DA's stand on his city needing to be clean. She kept her opinion to herself, but couldn't help thinking that nobody wanted to have this garbage in their area. Yet, if it were pushed out beyond their boundaries, they were fine. But it wasn't prudent to open that discussion.

"What you really mean is, we can't have it at all," Rhodes corrected. "Doesn't matter if it's in the cities or somewhere else, it will filter into the cities eventually."

Distracted, the DA said, "Yes, of course." He looked back at Sienna. "What do you need to get proof?"

"I'm not sure. I'm a programmer. But without access to the banks in question, I only have the spreadsheets to go on." She motioned to Rhodes. "He will be more help at this point. Or Levi's team at home."

"As I said earlier, some of these names are very high profile." He turned to look at Rhodes. "We can keep you out of this and the courts if we have actual physical proof. But if the methodology of how we got this information should ever be questioned, you might be required to come in as a witness."

She slumped in her chair and shook her head. "My reputation won't stand up in court."

Silence filled the room. His gaze narrowed, and he shot her a look. "Just what does that mean?"

She glanced over at Rhodes and shrugged. While she listened, Rhodes gave a short explanation of her history.

"As an end result, her name was muddied from all this."

The DA tapped the sheet of paper in front of them, then the box, and considered the issue. "I guess it's down to finding any hard facts, so it's not your word against theirs."

"Most of these people won't have very much registered under their names," she said. "If they're doing investment banking, offshore accounts, or anything like that, we'll find it with enough time. However, usually companies are involved, not an individual person. Shell corporations have doctored books to hide the profits that are moved. They wouldn't list arms dealing anywhere, unless they have legal licenses to do so."

"Sounds like you are the person I need right now," the DA said. "You specialize in banking security, which means you understand money." The DA pointed at one name on the list. "Find out everything you can about this man."

She looked down at the name. *J. R. Wilson.* She frowned. "Wilson's a very common name."

"He also owns and runs a company—a huge charity for refugee camps in the Middle East."

She slowly raised her gaze and said, "Which *is* perfect for gunrunning."

"Exactly." He gave her a quiet nod. "He also has headquarters in Dallas and Ghana. That's the connection to the African banks."

She looked over at Rhodes. "I don't know how long we're expected to be here, but I could get started now."

"Anticipating that you'd be willing to stay here and begin now," he said, "I have a brand-new clean white laptop. Every step you make will be tracked." He patted the box beside him. "And this holds everything we have on the company."

She looked from the box to the laptop and nodded. "It's the best way."

All gazes were on her, but still she hesitated.

In a low voice Rhodes whispered, "You don't have to."

She gave him a veiled glance, took a deep breath and opened the laptop. "How can I not?"

RHODES WATCHED HER. She'd been put in an awkward position she hadn't been ready for. He understood the DA wanted as much information as he could get from her, given any names on her decoded list were in this office, understanding there would be even more problems using those people in this investigation.

Bobby got up and walked to a coffee service on the sideboard. "Can I get anyone a coffee?"

"Yes, please," Rhodes answered for the two of them.

Bobby turned to look at Robert. "Do you want a cup?"

The DA shook his head, his gaze intent on Sienna. Rhodes wasn't sure he liked that either. She'd been put through enough for doing her job. She'd come here to work for Levi with a completely different expectation, and she had every right to avoid the same murky water she'd traveled before. Still she'd agreed. Stepping up when the need was thrust upon her.

On the other hand, she was gifted, had something everybody needed, so it was hard not to utilize her skills.

"I'll be nearby if you need anything else," Bobby said before leaving.

Two hours later, while the DA worked on his files here with them, she said, "Do you have a printer?"

Rhodes, sorting through the contents of the box, glanced at her. She looked a little pale. Then again, she hadn't had lunch either. Her breakfast had been various contents of Alfred's basket earlier. Or was her expression something more?

He had one hard-bound ledger in his hand. He opened it to find what looked like standard accounts. The interesting thing was, it was a paper copy. Didn't everyone do digital accounting these days? Still, it wasn't illegal. Unless they were keeping a second set of books. He replaced it in the box.

Robert lifted his head and stared at her in surprise. "I guess the laptop isn't connected to that printer, so email it to me and I'll print it."

She hesitated, and Rhodes understood why. "Robert, do

you have a small printer she could hook up here?" he asked. "To keep everything completely separated."

Robert stood up and said, "I'll go see." He buzzed for someone to come help but after five minutes with no answer, he got up and walked from the conference room and left Rhodes and Sienna alone.

Rhodes placed a fresh cup of coffee in front of her. She looked startled for a moment and accepted it gratefully. She picked it up and hugged the hot cup close to her.

Concerned, he asked, "Are you okay?"

She took a deep breath and nodded. But she didn't say anything. When he saw her white knuckles gripped the cup, he realized something was even more wrong than he expected.

"Can you tell me?" He glanced around the room and realized it was quite possible the room was bugged. It shouldn't be, but they had been led to this room in particular. Although they hadn't been left alone until he requested a printer, that didn't mean everything they said wasn't being taped and/or recorded. He could send her a text asking what was wrong, but if anybody saw them doing that, their phones could be confiscated before they left.

Feeling protective, he made a sudden decision and said, "Let's go back to the hotel. You can work there if you feel up to it. But really, you look like you should probably lie down."

He studied her face, and in truth, she did look ill. Her skin was white, and her forehead was moist, as if she had a fever. He frowned, walked over to the door and opened it. As he stepped into the outer hallway, the DA approached, accompanied by Bobby, carrying a small printer. Rhodes quickly explained the problem, motioning toward her.

Robert frowned. "Damn. Well, I guess you couldn't stay here much longer anyway. The office will close soon. Although I thought maybe we could keep working into the evening."

"We have a room booked for the night," Rhodes said. "Let me take her back so she can lie down. She might just need some fresh air. She also hasn't eaten since morning. If she feels better, we can come back."

The DA hesitated and glanced at Bobby, who shrugged. The DA turned back to Rhodes and said, "Take the laptop and box. If she feels like working, she can do so from there."

That was the best news he'd heard yet. Not giving anybody a chance to argue, he pointed at the printer and said, "Her reasons for needing that still applies. May we bring that too?"

Without a word Bobby handed it over.

Rhodes had his arms full. He laid the clean laptop inside the box and stacked the printer on top. With all that under one arm, he very gently snagged Sienna's elbow and lifted her to her feet.

"Come on. Let's get you into the room so you can lie down."

She gave both men a half-hearted smile and murmured, "Sorry."

"Don't be," Rhodes told Sienna. "I hadn't expected we'd be in the office that long. If I'd known, we'd have stopped for lunch."

As they walked out and went to the elevator, he wasn't sure if she was acting or really was sick, but her footsteps were getting fainter as they went along. By the time they got to the elevator, he was half supporting her, and now he was really worried.

The elevator was full. He got them both inside and down to the ground floor. Outside, still not knowing if she was physically ill or not, he led her to the truck and quickly got her inside and buckled in. On his side, he put the laptop and box in the backseat and hopped in. He considered whether anything had been placed inside his truck to monitor them.

And realized someone could have put a tracker on their clothing. He knew all too well how gifted some sleight-of-hand people were. It was also quite possible the laptop had something going on in it which she hadn't shared. Levi had already reserved the hotel suite for them. As Rhodes drove, he contemplated the options.

First was to get her safely inside. He quickly shifted her to the hotel room and had her stretched out on the bed. He made several trips back to the truck to grab their overnight bags and the box that contained the laptop and printer. On his last trip, he picked up the basket of food, the electronics from the compound, and the dashboard box where he had stowed his weapons—not allowed in the DA's building. Inside the room, he turned on the meter to see if any unexpected electronic devices were in the room. He did a full sweep, then came back to the clean laptop. Instantly the laptop caused the meter to buzz. He stared at it in shock.

She nudged him with her foot and said, "Exactly."

He lifted a finger to his lips, fished his phone from his pocket and stepped outside the hotel room. Still not happy with the distance, he walked to the parking lot where his truck was. There he stood and called Levi. He quickly explained what was going on.

"What? The laptop was bugged? That the DA gave you? You sure it wasn't just the fact that the document was being tracked?"

"No. She saw something. She immediately became ill or faked it. We're at the hotel now, and the new testing device Bullard sent us tells me the laptop is bugged. They know where we are. It doesn't change the fact that she needs a laptop to work on."

"Did you bring yours?"

"I've got the one that comes with the truck."

"See if she can use that. She can log on to the main server here. We need to get to the bottom of this and fast." Levi hung up, leaving Rhodes staring at the empty truck. He had taken the company laptop up to the hotel room with the other stuff. He walked back to the room, picked up the laptop from the DA's office, brought it back to the truck and locked it behind the driver's seat. Then back in the hotel room he once again tested for more electronic devices. The sweep was clean this time.

Laying down the testing kit, he said, "Okay. Now we can talk." He sat gently on the bed and leaned beside her, looking down at her. "First off, are you really sick? Or is this just a pretense?"

"Both," she said. "When I realized that laptop was recording our voices, I realized I was right back into the same damn thing I was in before. And that's when I felt sick."

"Right. Levi says to use my laptop to do whatever work you need to. Their laptop is locked in the truck."

She gave a sigh, rubbed her eyes and shifted her position so she was propped against the headboard.

"What else did you find?"

"The initials R.F. again."

He studied her as she tried to figure out who R.F. was.

"The DA's name has both those letters."

"Ah, hell." That was not good.

"Exactly. Either he wants this information so he can bury it or to figure out how to better hide his tracks, or there's a completely different R.F."

Rhodes reached for his laptop, flipped it open and placed it on her lap gently. "One of the hard rules of this kind of work is the fact that there's only one way to know how bad a scenario can get. You have to keep digging through the surface for the meat underneath. Just because R.F. is there, doesn't mean it's the DA's name being referenced."

"Three names were decoded. Or rather three sets of initials, because three of those patterns were just numbered accounts, which we can't easily access to find the corresponding names, and then we have the initials R.F."

He nodded. "We'll go on the assumption the DA's a good guy. But we won't take any chances, and we'll always keep in mind, if we find any proof he's not, it's an entirely different story."

"Then what do we do?" she cried. "He's the DA."

"That's easy. We go above him."

"And what if above him is corrupt too?" she asked, her voice bitter. "That's what happened to me. And when it all came back down, they blamed everything on me."

"I won't let that happen. You won't be too involved. You've been asked to come in and help out, that's it."

"In theory I understand that. But my heart still tells me to get the hell out and run in the opposite direction."

"You could look at this as an opportunity to leave all that behind. Because as soon as you step up and face it, it helps put your life back in control, like you're no longer a helpless victim. That you are the one with the power to turn it around."

She stared at him, fear in her gaze.

He tugged her into his arms. "Take it easy."

"It's not that easy ..." she began.

He just held her close, feeling the trembling inside, even though she was doing her best to hide it. So strong, and yet so fragile. "Of course it's not. You were railroaded last time. That's not the same thing here. But you do have the ability to put some of these people—who have been doing this for a long time—in jail. And maybe you won't find anything. You won't know until you start looking."

"He wants me to look into the company books, but ..." she reached over and lifted the same ledger he'd looked at in the office, "the tears from missing pages look suspiciously like the scanned pages Bullard sent us with its ripped edges."

"What are you saying?"

"I'm saying, the DA didn't give me the information I needed, but whether that was an oversight or deliberate, I don't know. There should be all kinds of information online and on paper to back this up and the accounting program they used on the laptop, but the only thing loaded here are the company books."

"We have to trust somebody." He opened his phone and quickly phoned Robert.

"She says she's missing a lot of information here. So, she can't check through the code to see what might be there. Are you sure it's all here?"

"Did she check the box? The answer is yes. It's all there, or it should be." There was a pause in his voice. "What do you mean, that's not all of it? I had our department look. I'll check with them to see if they still have anything." The DA's voice sounded muffled. "I'm walking over there right now.

I'll call you back in ten."

Staring down at his phone, wondering if he should notify Levi, Rhodes said, "Several others had the information first. He's gone to see if they still have any of the material. He thought it was all contained in the box and laptop."

She patted the box and said, "Not even close to what I'd expect."

His phone rang almost immediately. "My men said they put everything in the box. However, they digitalized everything first so we do have copies."

"Send us a digital copy via Levi. We can compare what's there versus what's in the box." His voice deepened as he added, "You might want to consider somebody in your office carefully removed a few things."

"That would be too obvious surely. John's the one who scanned in everything. Sending it now." And for the second time the DA hung up on him.

The email came in moments later, routed via Ice. Rhodes brought up the scanned ledger from the DA and flicked to the back. It was missing the same pages. He glanced at Sienna. "It does have missing pages. So quite possibly the scanned ones Bullard sent you belong in this ledger."

"So the question here is, how did those pages end up in Ghana and the ledger in Dallas?"

They smiled at each other. "J. R. Wilson," they said at the same time.

"This is great evidence of his involvement."

"Or someone who works for him," she corrected. "And guys like him are slippery. If they can pin it on someone else, they will."

"As you already know," Rhodes said quietly.

Chapter 7

"AS I ALREADY know," Sienna repeated his statement. "Yes. I thought I knew my coworkers. But they fooled me." She shook her head. "What is there for food?" She reached up a hand and rubbed her temple. "I'm feeling better. I don't know if it was the air conditioning there or the damn coffee, but I was pretty nauseated."

"We can order in, or check out the hotel restaurant."

Sienna glanced at the paperwork and laptop. "I'm not comfortable leaving this material here without us. So, delivery or room service."

He studied her for a long moment. "I saw a little Italian place around the corner when we drove in. Would you be okay if I left you long enough to get two dinners?"

"That would be perfect." She smiled at him. "And I really love Italian."

"I think you just love food of all kinds." He got up, turned to look at her and said, "Do not let anybody inside. And don't answer the hotel phone." And with that he started to leave, only to stop at the doorway, pivot and walk back. He leaned down and gave her a long, hard kiss. As he lifted his head, he whispered in a dark voice, "Stay safe."

When she could breathe again, she found him gone.

She leaned back against the headboard, grateful for the moment alone to catch her breath. He was a hell of a kisser.

And he cared. She smiled, knowing that regardless of this op or any others to come, she'd been right to accept Levi's offer.

Considering her growling stomach, she was also grateful a meal was coming but was a little more concerned about the fact that information was missing. It had all the hallmarks of someone laying the blame on her. Again. What she had was a clean set of books. And a ledger with some of the pages missing. All it did was make her suspicious. She wasn't an accountant per se. She was a programmer. She flicked open the laptop and looked at the company books again. It showed the last three years. It would take time to go through the multiple entries, so she picked a place to start. She flicked back to last summer and read through them, finding a lot of stationary and supplies, food, shoes, and clothing.

Then it was a charity. Was it asked to buy the stuff, or was it supplying it? It took her a while to figure out the pattern, but then it hit her. Way too many shoes were headed to Africa. She quickly highlighted every entry. And then every one listed as clothing. The figures were astronomical. Unless they were clothing thousands of people in a shelter or village, she didn't understand how these numbers could be so high. They were listed as expenses, and that didn't make much sense to her either because the company was running in the black. There were cheaper ways to buy things like this, she was sure.

As she searched for shipping and/or handling fees, something to ascertain that these products had actually been moved overseas to help somebody, she slowly got a picture of the company. Bringing up a webpage, she quickly researched the business, realizing they were indeed, digging wells, setting up schools, and supplying clothing to the villagers. They were proud of the fact they had put running water into four separate villages so far.

And everything made sense, except for the shoes. Every time she saw a picture of anybody at these villages, they were barefoot. On the other hand, most people wouldn't even blink if they were sending shoes over because, of course, they went together with clothes—but really only to the Western way of thinking. Many people in Africa didn't wear shoes by choice.

On a sheet of paper, she quickly jotted down some notes. The DA could easily ask for answers to some of these questions. As she kept searching through the months, going by location, most of the products had gone to the four villages. Which was all fine and dandy, but she didn't understand where the money was coming from. All these charitable donations originated overseas, and most of them were labeled in code. Invoice numbers with a single letter behind them.

And a few of them were suspiciously familiar.

But when she went to the box, nothing backed up those single-letter references. There had to be another set of books or something that tracked all these invoices. Everything cross-referenced. Business was all about checks and balances. And if this charity went through an elaborate scheme to hide money, it sure as hell wouldn't have done a sloppy job of it. Not at this level. She needed access to the bank's program. But if the company was smart, they'd have used multiple banks. Sure enough, a few months later, invoices showed up.

She continued through six more months, but it was mostly a repetition of the previous ones. The company appeared to be buying shoes and clothing from those going out of business and shipping them to several villages. Which made sense as to the quantities purchased—but not for the prices paid—except by now they should have warehouses of merchandise somewhere. Were they planning on stockpiling for other villages? She shook her head. There had to be an easier way.

But it wasn't her job to judge the validity of a company. Or how well it was run or the business practices behind it. All she knew was the banking program had been hacked and somehow involved this company.

As she moved forward within the books, she could see the company's focus had changed. Instead of clothing, they now bought tools, seeds, and small equipment. She approved. Much better to allow the villagers to help themselves than to just keep doling out charity.

Slowly she gained an understanding of the company's business practices.

When the hotel room door opened, she looked up with a start.

"Sorry it took so long," he said. "I would've called, but they said ten minutes, and instead it was twenty." He closed the door behind him and placed the bag on the bed. "They gave us several dishes and said we can make up individual plates."

She carefully replaced the material in the box, followed by Rhodes's laptop, and walked over to the bed. As she pulled out the dishes, the smell hit her. And that's when she realized just how absolutely, horrifically hungry she truly was. She hated to say that even her fingers were trembling.

"What's the matter?" He studied her with concern. He walked closer and picked up her hands, frowning. Then lifted one to his lips.

If he intended on that calming things down, well, it wasn't helping. But she also wasn't sure she wanted to move so fast. She'd been sucked into a whirlwind romance the last time. She wanted to go slow and make sure she knew who Rhodes really was. Attraction was one thing. But she didn't want an affair. She was hoping for the whole shebang.

"I guess I'm just really hungry," she said, loving the concern but not wanting him to worry. "And my blood sugar drops more and more lately, particularly if I don't eat on time."

"Are you diabetic?"

She laughed and pulled her hand free. "It's more than likely my iron is low. The doctor said I am not taking care of myself."

She sat down on the bed, grabbed a paper plate and dished up one-third of each of the three dishes. For the next ten minutes, there was silence as she ate. She lifted her head to see him thoroughly enjoying his meal too. He was an easy companion. Quick with decision-making, but happy to get her input, like dinner. "This is really tasty."

He nodded. "It smelled wonderful when I walked in."

"I just have no idea what it is."

He laughed. "Well, obviously, it's pasta. Some Italian-sounding name. But what I remember, they had roasted vegetables and a breaded meat."

At that she laughed. "I figured that much by myself."

He reached over, grabbed the receipt stapled to the paper bag and handed it to her. "Here, maybe it'll make sense to you.

But the items were written in Italian. And not much of it made any sense. She tossed it on the bed and said, "Doesn't matter. It's delicious."

"Did you find out anything while I was gone?"

"They made some bad business decisions early on. They

should have warehouses full of clothes and shoes by this point, but finally they now supply tools for these villages they're working with," she said. "They brought in fresh water for the people and have been teaching them how to garden for themselves."

"I approve of that."

"I do too."

"But what about warehouses full of clothes and shoes?"

"Honestly I have no idea. But they have all these purchases for them."

"Let's hope they were reasonably decent purchases, and they have handed them all out. What about income?"

"Most of it is donations. When the money comes in, and they have it sitting there, then they spend."

"Well, that makes good business sense. Most of us can't do it any other way."

"Exactly. So far I've not seen anything terribly odd."

"So that's good then. Finish so we can go home."

She shook her head. "Not quite."

He lifted his head and stared at her. "Sorry?"

She glanced over at him. "It's too clean."

Chewing, he slowly lowered his plate and studied her face. "So you suspect something is wrong here?"

"Let's just say I have questions. If the DA can get the answers, then potentially we're in the clear."

"If there's no profit—which, from what I understand you're saying, the money comes in, and they spend it all—so it goes out again."

"I'm sure buying the farming tools is good, but I can't guarantee what they're listing is actually what they're purchasing. Ten thousand shovels are listed in separate entries, but were that many picked up and delivered?"

"How big are the villages?"

"Isn't that the question?" She smiled at him. "Ten thousand shovels isn't a lot when you're talking about several being outfitted. It all depends on what they were doing and the population of the able-bodied individuals in each. We don't have facts and figures on the villages, and we don't know if they are buying that many because they got a better deal, and they'll always need them down the road."

He nodded. "I can see what you mean. What about the owner?"

"Nothing. No dividends were paid to him, and he's not withdrawing cash in any way, shape, or form."

"So he's clean. And that's who the DA wanted you to find more information on?"

"Yes and no. How he made his money is something I'd like to know."

"He shouldn't be making it from a non-profit charity."

"He probably draws a salary if he's working for the charity full time. The statistics of what those CEOs earn running some of the major charities across the states are pretty scary. A lot of them are making seven figures."

"That doesn't sound very charitable to me," he said with a frown.

"A lot of times the charity doesn't get the money it needs. It's too busy paying its staff." She shook her head. "A couple employees in the lower salary range are making less than fifty thousand a year."

"So they're handling all this themselves from this end."

"But I'm not seeing payments to any staff over in Ghana where the warehouses are. So, either they're all volunteers, they're dealing with another company. or are paying out cash. And maybe I need to access the banking software. They could be moving money that way in the background. Still, it gives me hope that we might leave tomorrow."

He took another bite and nodded toward the rest of the food. "When we're done eating, we can give the DA a call and see if he can get the answers for us."

"I was hoping you'd say that. I don't want to return to his office. Something is wrong there, but I can't put my finger on it. I just get nauseated and this closed-in feeling. I don't know what the hell made me sick, but I'm really not signing up for more of that air."

"And yet, I wasn't sick and neither Bobby nor Robert had any symptoms."

She nodded. "I can't explain it. But I had to listen to my own body."

"It could be just a case of nerves," he answered quietly. "Reminding you too much of your former job."

She nodded and turned her attention back to her plate.

When they finished dinner and cleaned up, he pulled out his phone. "Robert, she's gone through several months of the accounts and has a few questions. She can talk to you about them directly." He handed the phone to Sienna.

In a businesslike voice, she brought up the few questions she had about the company books. When she was done, she said, "Other than that, I'm not seeing anything at this point. It lacks information. These are very simplistic books. Only two people work for the company, and the person you asked me to keep an eye out for, J. R. Wilson, is not mentioned in any way. Some odd things are going on in the way the charity is run, but nothing that references him."

"I can call and get some of these questions answered," he said, but his voice was distracted as if buried in work. "It might not be until tomorrow morning."

"Let me know if you find anything else."

When she hung up, she handed it back to Rhodes. "He wants me to keep looking." She tapped the box and said, "I think Bullard should run this name for us. He could figure out if there's any property in Africa registered in the charity or owner's name, or even a family name."

"You think he's invested in Africa?"

"It would make sense, as that's where his charities are operating. Not to mention the warehouses."

"That's a call I can make." He opened his phone and said, "But I'll do it outside."

When he left again, she buried herself back in the laptop. The one thing about code she loved: everything was tracked.

"BULLARD, SEE IF you can find any information on a J. R. Wilson. He's a person of interest on that banking fraud case. We're currently in Dallas to see the DA. Checking out the charity he owns and runs here."

"*Wellness for Everyone?*" Bullard asked. "It's always been a bit dodgy. One thousand and one charities are here, everyone supposedly wanting to help." He paused then added, "But I can tell you that name comes with a warning."

"So we do have the right man?"

"I'll do some digging on this side, but I wouldn't be at all surprised."

Rhodes thought about that for a minute and said, "There was something in the early years about ordering clothes and shoes, but we're talking about hundreds of thousands of dollars' worth."

"It's possible it's legit," Bullard said carefully. "But not very probable. There's no point in buying clothes when a lot comes from the Western world and other countries for relatively small money, if not outright free. Just pay the shipping."

"According to Sienna, it's like they're stockpiling warehouses full of them."

"And if it is warehouses, it could be full of something completely different."

"And then it stopped. Instead the company bought tools, farming equipment, things like that."

"Which is what we would expect. And on the books it sounds like they had initial good intentions, making some bad decisions, and then quickly moved into an area more helpful for the people. But was it really clothing and shoes, or something else?"

"And of course, we didn't see any addresses where any of this stuff is stored."

"Actually I think I have an idea about that. But no way in hell can you get a warrant to go in and look. Not there." His voice slowed. "Given the connection, I think I'll send somebody around to do it. If I thought guns were in those warehouses, I'd be all over it."

After hanging up, Rhodes walked back into the hotel room to give an update, but instead of finding her back at work, it looked like she'd nodded off. Her eyes were closed, and her steady deep breathing came from her chest. "I'm not asleep," she whispered. "Honest."

He laughed. "Put it away. Tomorrow will come soon enough. We're waiting on Bullard to get back to us." He quickly explained their conversation.

She rolled over and stared at him. "It will be interesting to hear what he finds." She closed the laptop, tucked it into the box, replaced all the papers and moved it to the hotel desk. Then she returned to the bed, folded back the covers and crawled under them.

"Aren't you getting undressed first?"

"Too much work to do still," she muttered. "Besides, I won't get much sleep tonight. This is just a nap."

"It's almost nine o'clock. Better to sleep through the night."

She frowned, and he could see the ideas warring in her expressive face. Finally, she threw back the covers and growled, "Fine."

She grabbed her bag, pulled out some clothing and a small case and walked into the bathroom. When she returned fifteen minutes later, he was sitting on the bed with his laptop open, taking notes of what had happened during the day.

She was dressed in shorts and a tank top. She stumbled to the bed, threw herself under the covers, turned out the light on her side and muttered, "Good night."

He grinned. He never thought he'd want somebody who was prickly, but he liked her just fine. More than actually. He'd hoped for a little more interaction tonight, but given her state and the fact he'd already gotten a terrific response from his earlier kiss, it wasn't the time. ... She had to move at the speed she was comfortable with. He wanted her for a long while, not just for a good time. But he hoped for plenty of those through the years too.

"If only Jarrod could see you now," he muttered, laughing, but then remembered what her last lover had done to her. Well, he was no friend to betrayal, having experienced more of his own than he wanted to. But he'd made peace with it. Now he needed to help her do the same with hers.

"If you tell him, I'll be in a shitload of trouble."

"Would he really be upset?" Should he tell her about his conversation with her brother? Or wait until she was awake. The last thing he wanted to do was get involved in a discussion that would potentially upset her. She needed a good night's sleep. Today had been tough enough on her. Besides, they had time. And the journey was all that much sweeter, knowing where they were going.

"No idea. Not ready to walk that direction. The less he knows, the better. Same for his job. If I don't know he's going out on dangerous missions, then I don't worry. If he doesn't think I'm involved in something that'll mess up my life again, then he won't worry. It's a good deal all around."

"It's a bad one because it leaves you standing out in the cold alone."

"I'm used to it." On that note she pulled the blanket higher on her shoulders and sank deeper into the pillow. The conversation was over.

Chapter 8

S HE WOKE UP suddenly. Lying quietly in the center of the bed, Rhodes was atop the bedding beside her. His eyes were wide open. She leaned up on one arm only to have him immediately raise a hand to stop her from moving. Quietly she sank back down again and waited.

A shadow crossed in front of the hotel room window making her blood run cold. Outside their door stretched a lengthy deck that ran along the front of several hotel rooms. They were all separated by small fences, but in theory, anybody could hop across if they wanted to. She caught her breath again as the shadow retreated across the window once again. She waited anxiously for Rhodes to make some kind of move. But he didn't. Neither did he relax.

She was rather desperate for the bathroom. Didn't know if she dared take a chance. Finally, he dropped his hand, turned to look at her and said, "It's clear."

She raised her eyebrows but took his words at face value. She threw back the covers, slid off the bed and walked to the bathroom. Maybe it was nerves, maybe it was the stuff she'd been working on, but her sense of unease grew. After washing her hands and returning to the bedroom, she worried if she'd fall asleep again. She checked her cell phone to see it was four o'clock in the morning. She glanced over at him and said, "Do you think that shadow had anything to do with us?"

"Yes."

That was it, short, terse. A typical Rhodes's answer. He'd been a lot more amiable years ago. But then they hadn't been in danger back then. He had also been teasing and kind to her as a gawky teenager. She punched up the pillows against the headboard and crawled under the covers, then sat and stared at him. "Do we need to leave?"

He shot her a sharp look and shook his head. "Not yet."

She waited. But he didn't elaborate. "Are we waiting for something?" she asked in exasperation. "Are we waiting for this to get worse, for somebody to charge into the room and actually attack us?"

His gaze never stopped moving around the room as he checked out something. She didn't understand what he was looking for, but it seemed he was mentally cataloguing the contents of the room, wondering how fast they could get out.

"You want me to start packing?"

"How long would it take you?"

"Right now, running on adrenaline, five minutes."

His eyebrows shot up. "Make that two." He walked into the bathroom and closed the door.

She bounded out of bed and quickly got dressed. She hadn't brought much in the way of clothing with her, and had already packed the DA's material with Rhodes's laptop and the ledger inside the box of documents. So, it was complete and ready to go. If anybody was after her, chances were more than likely they'd want the ledger. Sienna knew something fishy was going on in those accounts, but they had to have the proof. The DA needed a forensic accountant to look in to this deeper. If they had digital copies of all the documents, it didn't really matter if the box of papers was stolen or not. But it would be much better to have it all.

Still there was no understanding the criminal mind these days. By the time Rhodes came out, she was putting her shoes on. She said, "I'm ready."

His gaze searched around the room, and he nodded. "You have stuff in the bathroom."

She walked in, packed the few toiletries she'd brought with her and added them to her backpack. "So where do we go from here?"

"It's too early to head to the DA's office, but several coffee shops are around."

"Okay. That works for me. Especially if we can bring in the laptop and work."

He glanced down at his watch and nodded. "It's 4:15. With any luck, there's an all-night café close by." He grabbed up his bag. "If I take the box, can you grab your bag?"

She snatched up her backpack, put it on her shoulders and grabbed the laptop, and together they headed out, locking up the hotel room behind them. He went by the registration desk and dropped off the key. Having already prepaid, it didn't matter when they left. Outside he led the way to the truck. There they stowed what they had and were on their way within minutes.

It felt odd to be up so early. Almost as if they were sneaking out of the hotel room so nobody could see them, but it wasn't a clandestine affair she was involved in. It was something a lot more dangerous.

Although an affair would be a lot more fun.

He drove from the lot and headed down the main street. Within minutes they found several good coffee shops. He pulled into the second one and parked. With Rhodes's laptop in her hands and a few of her notes, he locked up the truck, and they went inside to get coffee. "You want to eat?"

She shook her head. "Not right now. It's too early for that."

She settled back into the chair and opened the laptop. She was really too tired to review the material. Wasn't even sure what she'd found at this point. When the coffee was delivered, she closed the laptop again and pushed it off to one side, yawning.

"Did you get any sleep?" Rhodes asked as he reached across and covered her hand with his much bigger one.

She smiled. "Still the big-brother attitude?"

He raised his eyebrows at that. "Hey, I knew you back when," he said with a smile. "Besides, Jarrod's my friend."

"I'm no longer a little girl."

He settled back, gently pulling his hand away from hers.

She was kind of sorry she'd said anything. Something was so damn comforting about his touch. She doubled the cream in her coffee and stirred it.

"Did Jarrod say something to upset you before he left?"

She looked up in surprise. "Hell, no. Jarrod's a good guy. He knows he can trust me to have common sense."

"Have it about what?"

She gazed at him innocently over the rim of her cup. "Life, I guess." She smiled into her mug.

"Why is it I think you're laughing at me?" he asked.

She shrugged. "Jarrod gave me the same old warnings he's always given me. His friends are good, decent men, but they played fast and loose with women, so watch it. But he trusts me to make the right decision for me." She stared at him directly. "I got that warning ten years ago, and again a few days ago."

"Wow, I didn't know he still considered all of us that way."

"I don't think he does, but I think he was so used to giving that warning that it came out naturally as part of his habitual good-byes."

"That makes sense. I don't have a little sister to worry about, but I can see that being a prime concern."

"What he doesn't realize is that I'm an adult, and I won't have an affair with anybody I don't want to have one with," she said a little too strongly.

There was a sudden silence as he studied her. Then she realized she and Jarrod hadn't even discussed something along those lines. It wasn't like her brother was warning her off having sex; he was warning her off the men at the compound. That they couldn't be trusted to stick around longer than a one-night stand.

She shook her head. "And that's just an overly strong reaction of the younger sister having been told off for years and years on the same issue."

He laughed. "Whatever works."

She smiled. "You always did have that get-along-with-everybody attitude."

"I wondered how much you remembered from back then," he said curiously. "You never say much."

"What's to say? I met several of Jarrod's SEAL friends." She shrugged. "I've seen most of them over the years again too. This is the first I've seen of you since then though."

"Right. You sure don't look like you did back then. Cocky, skinny, braces, and carrot hair." He gave her a lopsided grin. "You were adorable. And are a beauty today."

Her gaze widened in surprise. "Well, I had a hero complex over you back then." She laughed. "I got rid of the braces, but sometimes I still put my foot in it."

He grinned. "I think we all do. That's not a skill you outgrow easily."

The waitress came back and asked, "Do you want to order anything to eat?"

Sienna shook her head. "Just more coffee for me, please."

She listened as Rhodes gave a similar answer. The atmosphere had warmed with their confessions. It gave her hope. She stared out the window, seeing the world around her lighten up slightly. That could've just been because her eyes were more adjusted, but it seemed like daylight was finally kicking nighttime into the background.

"Can we go home today, do you think?" she asked, pulling out a notepad. "I have a few points for the DA to look in to, but there's not a whole lot here."

"In that case, yes, we can go home."

She brightened. "Good."

"Glad to hear you consider the compound home."

"It took a while. After the attacks, I wondered what I'd gotten myself into. But I quickly realized Jarrod knew most of you and that somehow I'd been lucky to end up there. But since then, just sitting back and watching everybody go through their own personal relationship issues, it's been something else to handle."

Rhodes laughed. "Isn't that the truth? Levi and Ice, Stone and Lissa …"

"Merk and Katina," she added with a laugh. "Those two were destined to be together. I can't imagine how they even broke up last time."

"You might've felt differently if you'd been the one in

the Las Vegas wedding."

She grinned. "Good point."

"You are okay staying at the compound?" he asked, his gaze intent, warm.

Warmer than she'd seen before. Instead of making her uncomfortable, she wished they were alone. Still this bubble was intimate. The moment special. She gave him a slow smile. "For the moment. The work is interesting. Lots to learn and do, and I feel safe there."

"All good reasons."

"And, of course, I like the people." She batted her eyes at him playfully. "Some more than others."

OVER TWO HOURS later, Rhodes put down his empty coffee cup. "Let's go." He tapped his watch and said, "The DA's office will open soon. If we get there soon enough, maybe we can leave early. We could be home just after lunchtime."

That brought a smile to her face. He watched as she quickly packed up the little bit of material she had with her, drank the last of her coffee and stood up. "I'm leaving the laptop here while I go to the ladies' room."

He watched her go. That long, lean, gawky body had turned into a voluptuous woman with legs that seemed to never quit.

He wondered if Jarrod really did believe all of them were the *love 'em and leave 'em* types. Rhodes could understand the warning ten years ago, but it hardly applied now. Not with all his buddies getting hooked up, and those relationships made the place sound more like a love compound than an actual security one.

While he waited, he paid the bill. When she still didn't

return, he checked his watch and realized she'd been gone ten minutes. He frowned. That wasn't terribly outlandish, but if she wasn't back soon, he'd bust down that damn door and haul her out. He picked up the laptop and her notebook, pocketed the receipt from the register and made his way to the ladies' room. He knocked on the door and it pushed open easily. The room was empty, as were the four stalls.

He stepped back out again and searched the restaurant. Where the hell was she? He glanced at the window in time to see a small van leave the parking lot. Instantly he knew something was wrong. He bolted outside, checked the parking lot to make sure she wasn't waiting for him, raced to his vehicle, dropped the items inside and headed after the van. He jammed his phone onto the dashboard mount and called Levi. As soon as he came on, Rhodes said, "Sienna's gone missing."

He explained what happened and that he was chasing a white van but had no way to know if it had anything to do with her disappearance.

"Did you check the other washroom? Did you check everyone in the restaurant?" Ice asked. "If the place was busy, she could have used the men's room."

"The restaurant barely had a few people, and all the stalls were completely empty. Something's happened to her."

He knew it inside. His gut clenched. He unlocked his hands from gripping the steering wheel, his knuckles still white. Up ahead he could see the van as it went through several lights. Not giving a shit about the traffic speed, he gave the truck more gas and pulled up as close as he could to the van.

As if suddenly realizing they were being followed, the

van's driver crossed three lanes of traffic and took a left on the next street. It also went through a red light, leaving Rhodes in the middle of the intersection until the cross-traffic passed.

He quickly followed and turned down yet another street. No sign of the van. He drove slowly up and down it, then backtracked, looking for an alleyway, a garage, or something. Only two of the houses had a garage. He went around the back of the place but found nowhere for the van to hide.

Around the front again, he caught sight of one young guy standing outside on the front step. That could easily be him. As Rhodes passed the second house with a garage, he watched a woman and children walk out the front door. Immediately he made a U-turn and headed back to the first house. The man was no longer outside.

Rhodes parked in the driveway so they couldn't leave. He sent Levi a text with an update. He made it look as if he was heading around the back of the house. Instead he backtracked and snuck inside the garage via the side door.

Bingo. There was the van. He opened the doors, looking for any proof Sienna had actually been inside. The last thing he wanted was to barge into a house and terrorize a family who had nothing to do with her kidnapping.

Unfortunately the van offered nothing helpful.

At the back door, he peered through the window but found no sign of anybody inside. There had been a guy on the front step, but Rhodes didn't know where he'd gone. Rhodes opened the house door quietly and slipped inside. Stairs to the second story were right in front of him. With a quick glance around the stairwell, not seeing anyone there, he crept up the stairs.

He checked all the bedrooms, and in the last one he

found Sienna tossed onto a bed. Her mouth was taped; her hands and feet tied. She appeared to be unconscious. Still no sign of the person, or persons, who had taken her. Hearing a sound below him, he quickly hid in the closet.

Two voices traveled up the stairs. "Are you sure we should've taken her?"

"We didn't have much choice. They were heading back to the DA's office. You heard them."

Rhodes frowned. That meant whoever had taken her had been in that restaurant with them. A couple young punks sat two tables over, but he hadn't paid them any mind as they'd been sitting there drinking coffee and playing games on their cell phones. They hadn't shown any interest in her or him. Apparently he'd been wrong. They seemed to know exactly what Rhodes and Sienna's plans were.

"I still don't understand what difference it makes."

"They're afraid that whatever paperwork she has will implicate one of the bosses," the other replied.

"So why didn't we just steal the boxes?"

"Don't be daft. Everything's digital nowadays."

"And so what the hell difference does it make if we have her or not?"

"Leverage."

"Oh."

Rhodes watched through the slats of the closet door as two men walked over to Sienna. "Wake up, bitch."

Sienna didn't make a sound. The same guy hauled his arm back and smacked her across the face. Her head snapped from one side to the other and then rolled gently until it came to a stop. She never made a sound.

"How hard did you hit her?"

Inside Rhodes's anger built. They'd knocked her out,

and now they couldn't even wake her up? As soon as he got her out of here, she was heading straight to the hospital. No matter what she said.

"I didn't touch her. It's not my fault when I grabbed her that she slammed her head against the window. It made her easy to deal with though." The two guys backed up slightly. "You think we should tell anybody?"

"Hell, no. Let's not bring that type of trouble down on our heads just yet."

The two young men walked out of the bedroom when one of their phones rang. "It's the boss," said the kid.

Staring through the slats, Rhodes saw the kid on the phone wore a red shirt and the other a light gray hoodie. Honestly they looked so similar they could be brothers. They were both about five foot ten, skinny, with jeans that barely hung on their hips. Rhodes shook his head. What the hell had he and Sienna stumbled into?

The one in red spoke into the phone. "No, we've got her." He glanced over at his cohort and held up his hand. They high-fived each other. "No problem. We'll take her to the rendezvous point." He looked at his partner as his grin widened. "Sure, no problem."

He clicked his phone off. "We're supposed to take her down to the warehouse."

"Oh, shit. We just hauled her ass up here. Why didn't he call a few minutes earlier, and we could have just kept on driving," the hoodie guy said in disgust.

"Doesn't really matter. What the boss says, we do."

The hoodie guy looked over at the bed and said, "Shit."

Rhodes knew that carrying her upstairs had not been easy for these two scrawny teenagers. He watched as they walked over and manhandled Sienna off the bed to the floor, repositioned their hands and picked her up, slowly carrying her down the stairs.

Rhodes stepped out of the closet and waited until they went around the corner. They'd learn soon enough they couldn't leave without his vehicle being moved. As the guys went to the garage, Rhodes headed out the front door. He called Levi and the cops. He waited until the two had her at the back of the van inside the garage and followed. As soon as they lowered her to the ground, he took out the first one with a headlock. Only there was a brittle snap, and the kid went limp. Checking that he was unconscious, Rhodes dropped him to the floor. The second guy looked at Rhodes in shock.

"Who are you? Where did you come from?" His gaze landed on his partner on the floor, and he screamed. "Oh, my God! Did you kill Joe?"

Rhodes grabbed the kid and slammed him against the van, his arms pinned behind him and his head flattened against the side of the vehicle. "Maybe. Not that I planned it that way. What the hell did you expect when you kidnapped someone? A slap on your wrist?"

The kid started to cry. "You killed my brother."

He struggled in Rhodes's arms, but he seriously had no freedom to move and even less strength. No wonder it had taken the two of them to pick up Sienna.

Rhodes again slammed the kid against the van. "And you'll get the same treatment if you don't shut up."

The kid subsided. Rhodes glared at him as he pulled cuffs from his back pocket and quickly clipped the kid's wrists together. "*Jesus.* Kidnapping is a federal offense. Did you really think you would get away unscathed?"

"We weren't really kidnapping her," the kid said. "The

boss just asked us to bring her down, and she didn't want to go."

"Hence the term *kidnapping*, when you pick up people against their will. You've tied her up, knocked her unconscious, and hauled her out of that restaurant into your vehicle. Where the hell do you think you are going from there? I believe it's jail. If you live that long."

The guy's eyes widened as he stared at Rhodes in horror. "Oh, no, no, no, no, no. No jail for me. I won't survive it."

Rhodes could believe that. "The only way you might cut some of that jail time short, or get into an easier one, is if you cooperate fully."

Immediately the color drained from the kid's face. "You might put me in jail," he said, "but the boss'll kill me if I tell you anything." At the sound of sirens he trembled. "Oh, my God! I'm so in trouble."

"You'll be in even more when the boss finds out you've been picked up by the cops because he'll assume you turned on him. Your life is now forfeited anyway."

He stared at Rhodes, the horror in his eyes turning them almost black. "You don't understand these people. They have very long arms. They can also kill me in jail."

"Welcome to the criminal world," Rhodes snapped. Shoving the kid ahead of him, he quickly hit the button to open the double doors of the garage. And that's when the kid saw Rhodes's truck. "You were already on to us. You followed us from the restaurant?"

"Yes." Rhodes nodded. "I certainly did."

Two black-and-white police cars pulled up behind his truck. Rhodes quickly pulled out his ID and hauled the kid over to one of the men. But he didn't let him go.

An ambulance pulled up a few minutes later. He waited

until Sienna was checked over, then her still form loaded into the ambulance. He hated to leave her, but he also couldn't trust the cops. Before they could take possession of the prisoner, he phoned the DA's office and talked to Robert.

After that, things moved at a slightly different pace. Another vehicle arrived, and the DA himself got out. He took one look at the kid and said, "Take him in for questioning. Rhodes, I suggest you come with us." He glanced at the ambulance, now heading off down the street. "Will she be okay?"

"As for these assholes, he's the one who knocked her out," Rhodes said bitterly. "If you could just leave me alone with him for a few minutes ..."

The kid screamed, "He killed my brother. You can't let him anywhere near me."

The DA looked at Rhodes.

He shrugged. "I didn't kill him. Just rendered him unconscious."

The kid stopped and stared at him. "You told me that you killed him."

Rhodes smiled. "I lied."

He got into his vehicle and followed close behind the DA and his prisoner. No way was he letting this kid out of his sight. The DA seemed to understand. They drove to the police station and very quickly were in an interrogation room.

The DA said, "We must handle this officially."

Rhodes nodded. "I agree with that. But I need to know who the hell is after Sienna to put a stop to this fast. Get me a name. I'll take care of the rest." His voice was hard, his glare bitter. He wasn't letting up until he had that name.

Sienna had gone missing on his watch, and he'd never forgive himself for that.

Only the kid didn't want to talk. Between the cops and the DA, he just sat there and glared at them. In frustration, the three law enforcement officers got up and walked out.

Rhodes had been watching from the observation window. He said in a low voice, "Let me talk to him."

The officers immediately protested. Robert smiled and said, "You could scare anybody. Go ahead. You got five minutes. But remember, the entire thing is recorded, so stay on this side of the line. We can't have this case fall apart."

Rhodes walked in and headed straight for the kid.

The kid shrieked, jumped up from the chair and ran to the back of the room. "You can't touch me. The cops will keep me safe."

"The cops might, but only long enough to get the information we want. I already put word on the street you're talking."

"But I haven't said anything," he cried out in protest. "You can't lie like that."

"What universe do you live in, kid? Do you think this is some punk-ass game you played in high school? People are dying here. And you'll be one of them if you don't smarten up."

And suddenly the kid realized he really was in trouble. "You don't understand. If they think I'm tattling, they could kill me."

"And *you* don't understand. The minute you were picked up by the cops, they assumed you *were*, so you're dead anyway. You and your brother, Joe."

The kid walked over to the chair and slowly sank back down. "Oh, my God," he said. "You're right. I have no way out of this."

"Only one—cooperate fully with the cops. With any luck you and your brother will get a lighter sentence, and you might actually still have a life after this. If you don't, well, no promises."

Rhodes turned and walked out, slamming the door behind him. As he left, the kid yelled, "Wait, wait. I want to talk."

He nodded to the cops. "That's your cue." He stormed over to the side window and glared out at the morning sun. He still wanted to wring the little chickenshit's neck.

The DA said, "A little brutal but effective."

That startled a laugh from Rhodes. "Yeah, that's me, right down the line." He turned to study the man they'd come to help. "The files and your laptop are in my truck. I'll get them for you, and then I want to know who ordered the attack on Sienna."

One of the cops came out and walked over to them. "He wants to make a deal."

The DA said, "That's my cue." He turned back to Rhodes. "If you'll bring in those materials, that'd be great. I presume you're heading to the hospital right now?"

Rhodes nodded. "Until we pick up whoever it is that ordered the kidnapping, she's not safe. Not even there."

As the DA walked in to make a deal with the punk kid, Rhodes raced to his truck, pulled out the box of information the DA had given him and carried it to the observation room. As he entered the outer room again, the DA was talking with the police officers.

The DA took one look at the box and smiled. "Okay, we got names and addresses. We're putting together a tactical team to go after them." He hesitated and said, "I know you'd like to, but I can't have you take part in that."

"Damn." He shrugged. "You do your thing. I'll go to the hospital and protect Sienna. I let that asshole get at her once. Can't let that happen a second time."

"You're not responsible for this," the DA called as Rhodes headed to his truck.

"I'm not, but I am." And Rhodes thought, *That's just the way life is.*

Chapter 9

S HE WISHED TO hell the noise—moaning—would shut up. It was really giving her a headache. She shuddered and tugged the blankets higher up on her shoulders. She had no idea where she was, but everything hurt.

"Sienna?"

A gentle finger stroked across her cheek. She struggled to open her eyes. When she finally did, everything was blurry. But the moaning had stopped. Thank God for that.

As she stared ahead, a fuzzy rendition of Rhodes's face came into view. A second later, she could actually see him clearly.

"Hey." He leaned over and kissed her very gently on the temple.

Her eyelids fluttered closed. "What … happened?"

"You went to the washroom in the restaurant and met up with two punks who tried to persuade you to go with them." His tone was dry. He gingerly sat on the edge of the bed and reached down to gently cradle her hands in his.

She stared at him in surprise as the memories tumbled in and around each other. "One wore a hoodie and the other had a red T-shirt on."

He nodded. "Brothers. Just young kids. They were ordered to pick you up, if they got a chance, and they took it at the restaurant."

"And, of course, you rescued me, right?" She gave him a knowing smile. And she was very grateful to have missed the whole damn thing.

"It took me a few minutes," he said gravely. "I saw them take off and gave chase. But I couldn't guarantee you were inside the van. I found it in a garage at somebody's house. When I got inside, you were upstairs tied up on a bed."

She stared at him in shock. "I don't remember any of that."

He bent down and kissed her on the nose. "Good. Another set of nightmares you won't have to worry about."

She rolled over and tried to sit up, crying out in pain. Her hand instinctively went to her head. "Did they hit me over the head or something?" She groaned and realized that the moaning she'd heard earlier was probably coming from her. How embarrassing was that?

Using his strong arms, he slowly propped her up against the pillows. She felt slightly better, but it took a moment for the booming in her head to stop. "Did you catch them?"

He gave a half snort.

She smiled with her eyes closed. "Of course you did." No question about it. She was here with him.

"I captured them. The second I did, I got the police and DA involved. Robert was there when they collected them, to make sure we didn't lose them to a crooked cop, and now they're cutting a deal with him."

"That's actually the best thing we could've hoped for," she said with a smile. "Does that mean we can go home now?" She tried not to whine, but she didn't want to stay. "I really don't want to spend another night in a hotel, worrying someone is breaking in."

"Since you're awake, we won't have to check you into

the hospital, I hope. You're still in the emergency room. As soon as the doctor clears you, I'll take you to the station to give a statement. Then we can leave."

Her shoulders sagged a bit. "That sounds horrible. I was thinking maybe you could just pick me up, put me in the truck and drive me home." Her eyelids slowly lowered again at the thought of all that extra movement. "Everything hurts."

"The kid says he didn't hit you, that you slammed into the window. You were probably fighting them."

"If I did, I must have taken the damn window latch to my brain," she muttered. "I didn't even have much time to react. It just seems like my world went black right away. And if they knocked me out, why the hell does everything hurt?"

He grinned. "You really won't like this part."

When he didn't continue speaking, she finally rolled her head slightly to look into his eyes. "What part?"

"They were both very skinny teenagers, not a pound of muscle between them. They had difficulty lifting you."

She stared at him in outrage.

He laughed. "So I am pretty damn sure they must've dropped you on your butt to shift their grip many times. I was there as they tried to carry you from the bedroom and down the stairs. They might've bumped a few body parts going around corners too." He chuckled. "And before you ask, I had no opportunity to get you away from them without putting you in more danger. The last thing I wanted to do was take them out and have you roll down the stairs and break your neck."

She gave a tiny shrug. "I can understand that but damn ..."

He laughed, bent down and kissed her. This time on the

lips. "I'm just so damn glad to see you alive and well," he said cheerfully. "Although I probably shouldn't kiss you with you being Jarrod's sister."

"Would you stop always shoving Jarrod into my face?" she snapped. "He's not here, and he's got nothing to do with us."

"Are you sure?" He stared at her with a steady gaze. "He's your big brother, and he cares about you."

"And you're his friend, and you care about me too." She smiled. "You just won't admit it."

His eyebrows rose at her words. "Of course I do. You're Jarrod's sister."

He had turned the tables on her very neatly. She glared at him. "Is that all I am to you?"

He frowned, his gaze dropping away.

"Right. I'm not. So drop the excuse. My brother isn't here, and he's not my guardian. I'm an adult. I can do what I want with whom I want."

"And what is it you want to do?" he asked, lowering his head to kiss her again.

"Right now I want to feel better." When she could, she whispered, "And that means getting the doctor to give me permission to leave, getting to the goddamn police station, giving my statement and going home."

She shoved the blankets back and slid her feet to the floor. With more bravado than strength, she stood up and clung to the bed rail. "But first I have to make it to the bathroom."

Instantly he was at her side, holding out a hand. Grudgingly she accepted it, and using him as a crutch, made her way to the bathroom. At the doorway, he stopped and raised an eyebrow, looking down at her. She shook her head ever-so-slightly.

Even that little bit of movement made her wince. "I'll be fine."

"You'd be 'fine' even if you're not because no way in hell would you ask for help, right?"

"Right." And she shut the door in his face.

"STUBBORN," HE SNAPPED.

From the other side of the door came her response, "Yep, get used to it."

He shook his head. "No way to get used to that," he called back. He could hear the muffled snort from the inside of the bathroom, and grinned.

He pulled out his phone to check for messages, wondering if he should say anything to Jarrod about his sister being attacked. But Jarrod was on a mission, out of touch. Still, if Jarrod did get it, that would be fine. At least he'd be in the loop. Making a sudden decision he pulled up his buddy's number and sent him a text.

Sister was attacked. She's okay. We're on it.

Instantly a response came flying back.

WTF? Make sure you get the asshole.

Rhodes laughed.

I already did. At least two of them.

Is she really okay? Are you standing guard? I know how much she means to you. It was impossible to miss.

Rhodes winced at that last line of text. Was it really that obvious? The attraction had always been strong. It was easy to walk away when she was a gangly teenager—*completely* out of bounds. But now those had changed, and the markers moved. Nothing was stopping them from having a relationship except that sense that she was still out of bounds. She was the sister of one of his best friends. *Really*, he thought, *he should get a goddamn reward for being a good guy here. He hadn't made a move. And he knew a lot of guys would have.*

She's also your sister, Rhodes texted. **I've always honored that.**

Don't be stupid. Sienna has the right to make her own mistakes and go after what she wants. If that happens to be you, then welcome to the family, at least temporarily. If it isn't you, sorry. But there is one constant here. If you go after her and hurt her, I'm coming after you.

At least after that text was a small happy face to let Rhodes know that, although Jarrod wouldn't take kindly to Rhodes hurting his sister, there was at least some understanding of relationships. He loved the double standard though, where it was okay for Sienna to hurt him, but if he were to turn around and hurt her, well, he'd have to answer to Jarrod. Still, if Rhodes had a little sister, he'd be the same way. Now, as he thought of the damn good men he worked with, he realized a little sister of his would be damn lucky to be with any one of those guys. Not one of them took a relationship lightly, nor would any deliberately hurt a woman, and never would they hit one. There was something to be said about knowing your buddies would take you to task if you even considered abusing anybody.

The door opened behind him, and he spun around. Sienna took the first step forward, and Rhodes gave her a helping hand. Whether she had been pinching her cheeks or was just feeling better, the color had returned to her skin, and she stood strong.

"You're looking better."

"I feel better too." She walked slowly to the bed and sat down on the edge. "Can we leave now?"

"Let me find a doctor," he said. "See if we can get him to sign off on you leaving."

She raised her eyebrows. "Let me rephrase that. I'm leaving. Are you coming with me?"

He stopped and stared. "You really don't like authority, do you?"

"I find when you phrase a question the wrong way, it gives people the option to do the wrong thing," she said. "I'm not an emergency. I'm taking up a bed. I'm no longer unconscious, and I'm feeling much better. Yes, I have a head wound, but with careful behavior and someplace quiet to rest, we both know I'll feel better. And I don't want to be here. I was kidnapped once. Let's not give them an opportunity to get me again." She turned and studied the room. "I'm covered in blood, and I don't see my purse. Any idea if I came in with my personal effects?"

"Your purse came with you."

"Oh, good. The damn cards would've been such a pain to replace. You think we'd come to the point where we have chip IDs under the skin or something."

He laughed and reached under the bed, pulling out a plastic bag. He upended it on the bed. "These are your personal effects."

She grabbed her purse and pulled out her hairbrush. She

checked that her wallet and its contents were there and slung the whole thing over her shoulder, brushing her hair quickly, which just snagged on the dried blood there. "Let's go." And she walked past him out to the reception area.

There she handed over her insurance card and waited while the paperwork was completed. When she turned around, paperwork and receipts in hand, he held out his, offering support. Instead of putting her arm through his, she slipped her hand into his and laced their fingers.

"Can we go home now?"

"Police station first if you're up to it."

She nodded. "Make it fast."

It was fast but still took over an hour. As he helped her back to the truck, he found the DA's laptop he'd stashed there the night before. Shit. "Robert, she's out of the hospital but pretty woozy. And I found your laptop in the truck. I missed it earlier."

"Can you bring it back before you leave?"

"Yes, we can do that much." He walked around, got in the driver's side and started the engine. "The DA wants me to drop off their laptop. Then we're free to go."

"Perfect." And as if washing her hands of the whole issue, she curled up in the far side and laid her head against the glass. Then she closed her eyes.

He wanted to rush back to the hospital. He understood her point about not staying there, but she didn't look like she was strong enough to have left either. The walk outside had been enough to finish her. "You want to stay in town or are you up for the long drive home?"

"I'll sleep along the way," she said. "That's exactly what I need right now."

It was pretty hard to argue with that. He pulled in the

front of the DA's building and said, "I don't want to leave you out here alone."

She opened her eyes and turned to look at the building, then over at him. With a heavy sigh she nodded. "No, I can't say I want to be alone either right now. But getting up there to the DA's office, … well, that's looking like a little bit too much work."

But she opened the door and slowly got out. He opened the extended cab, pulled out the laptop, then locked the doors. He stepped beside her and said, "Grab my arm. We'll take the elevator straight up."

They walked inside and headed for the elevator. By the time they got to the DA's office, she was looking a little on the weaker side yet again. But as soon as they walked in the office and people stared at her, her back stiffened, and her grip on his arm tightened. She had grit. He loved that.

Robert rushed over. "How are you feeling? I am so sorry we got you involved in this."

"It wasn't exactly the highlight of my day," she said with a wan smile. "But you couldn't have known they would come after me either."

They walked into the office where Rhodes set down the laptop near the box of documents. "Everything she found is still there, and of course, traceable. And the paperwork I delivered earlier."

The DA shook their hands and said, "Much appreciated. I'm so sorry about what happened though." He offered them a chair. "Do you want a quick cup of coffee? Can I get you anything?"

He was going to refuse but Sienna said, "A cup of coffee would be nice."

He looked at her and saw she was determined to make

this as normal a visit as possible. Besides, the caffeine would be good. Neither of them had had a cup in the last few hours.

The DA spoke to somebody just outside the room. He directed them to the chairs in the boardroom around the long table. They discussed the case for several minutes over coffee.

"With the information we have from the young kidnappers, we can trace the people who hired them." He was effusive in his thanks. "I'm just so sorry this has come at the price it has."

Silently Rhodes agreed. But sometimes shit happened. What could you do but reach for the toilet paper?

Chapter 10

A S MUCH AS she hated to admit it, she was feeling the effects of her kidnapping. She didn't know how long she'd been in the hospital, but when she checked the time and saw it was almost four o'clock in the afternoon, she realized just how much longer the day would still get.

But she'd been honest when she said she was likely to sleep most of the way. She was also getting hungry. Maybe that was a good sign. Although she was afraid if she ate anything, it would come right back up.

They had a second cup of coffee and continued going over some of the information they found. She also learned the kids who kidnapped her had made a deal with the DA. She didn't have a problem with that. She was more concerned about getting the people above them. What she didn't want was to have anybody coming after her again.

It was thirty minutes in when the DA stood up and said, "We're very grateful to you, Sienna. I'll let you be on your way. The office is closing in a few minutes too."

An alarm ripped through the building.

She quickly put her cup down and stood. Her hand went to her head as the sudden movement brought on the pounding inside again. "What the hell is that?" she asked. She reached out for Rhodes immediately and found his arm wrapping around her, holding her close.

He looked at the DA and said in a hard voice, "What does the alarm mean?"

The DA's expression showed shock, bewilderment. "I don't think I've ever heard it before, but it's a lockdown."

"Lockdown?" she asked in a faint voice. "As in we can't leave?"

He nodded. His hand immediately went to the phone. Picking it up, he put in a call to security. There was a short exchange. "Security said they've had a viable threat called in from one of the other offices. They apologize, but lockdown mode is necessary until I can verify what's happening."

"Wouldn't it be better if we were all allowed to leave first?" she asked. The last place she wanted to be was here.

But Rhodes made it very clear. "The only reason they wouldn't let us leave is if they're afraid this person would escape with the crowd." His voice fell off as he considered the implication. He looked at the DA, then back outside. "Call security back and see if this person is holding anybody hostage in the building."

The DA immediately picked up the phone again and called security. "This is the DA. I want more details. Specifically, I want to know exactly what the threat is right now."

He stood rigid; his voice never changed, but his gaze immediately zinged to Rhodes. "One gunman or two?"

After a few more harsh words, he hung up the phone. "Two gunmen were seen on the floor below us. Security was called by somebody who saw them on the elevator. The lower three floors have been emptied of employees. Only our security guards are left. We're on the fifth floor. The gunmen were seen on the fourth. No sign of them now. Plus, there's been no contact with or from them."

Sienna slowly sat back down. "Is it me they're after?" She waved her hand at the box of materials on the table. "Or the information you have?"

"Both prisoners, the kids, were taken downtown to lockup earlier. They left maybe an hour ago. But we did it on the sly. Just in case ..." the DA said. "If that's who they're after, they are out of luck. If, however, they are after me, or even you two, ... then it's not so good for us."

She glanced at Rhodes. "Are you armed?"

He shook his head. "I have weapons locked in the truck."

"He wouldn't have been allowed to bring them into the building," Robert said. "Our security system wouldn't let him pass through the metal detector if he'd been armed."

"Well, it didn't work then, did it?" she snapped. "Apparently we have two gunmen inside downstairs, while the good guys aren't allowed to carry weapons to defend themselves." She leaned her head back and rubbed her face gently. "I knew we shouldn't have come inside."

There wasn't much anybody could say to her. Rhodes reached his hand down and grasped hers. "It'll be fine."

She opened her eyes and stared at him. "How the hell can you say that?"

"Because I'm getting you out of here." He looked at the DA. "Both of you, you're targets." He glanced at the box of paperwork and laptop. "Do you have a place to lock that up safely?"

Robert hopped to his feet, walked to the side filing cabinets and opened the bottom one. They put the laptop in and pulled the paper out of the box, filling the drawer. He locked it up, pocketed the keys and left the empty box with the lid on the table.

With Rhodes ushering them both toward the door, they quickly moved through the series of offices.

Sienna glanced around as she walked. "It looks like most of the people have left already."

"The offices closed a few minutes ago."

"So maybe the gunmen wanted that to be the case."

They shouldn't have stayed for coffee.

Still, it was too damn late. Like so much of her life. She couldn't believe she was in this situation. Talk about going from shit to shit. Still, she trusted Rhodes. He'd saved her once; she figured he'd do it again.

Although that was a lot of pressure to put on one man. And no matter how good anybody was at any point in time, everyone's luck ran out sometime.

THIS WAS NOT the end of the day he'd planned. It wasn't even the afternoon he'd hoped for. They should've just left. In fact, she should've stayed in the vehicle and he could've come back down after delivering the box. But the world was full of *should haves.* Now they were stuck in the building with gunmen. And no way in hell those men weren't after either Sienna, Robert, or both.

He wished he had his weapons though. He'd already have these two gunmen taken out. And Sienna's safety was primary. He needed a weapon, which meant he had to take one off the gunmen. He opened the door to the hallway, calling back to Robert in a low whisper, "How many exits are there?"

"There's the stairs and a service elevator. Plus, the three main ones."

"Where's the service one?"

"We can't access it from here. Have to go to the floor below. This was an add-on to be a rooftop deck and God only knows, a garden, I guess. They decided to close it in for offices. So the service elevator only goes to the fourth."

Rhodes turned and looked at him. "We have to take the stairs or the elevator down one floor so we can grab the service one?"

Robert nodded.

That was the stupidest of all stupid ideas. But Rhodes had certainly heard a lot worse. Development projects had construction issues, all covered up in a pretty layer of drywall and paint.

"Is it safe to leave?" Sienna asked behind him.

"The one thing you can count on is if they're looking for you, they'll go room by room. If we stay here, they would eventually find us."

"I vote for escape," Robert said.

"I do too." Sienna added, "I have no intention of sitting here like livestock going to the slaughter. If they want a piece of me, then they'll have to fight for it."

As much as he liked her attitude, she didn't have enough in her right now to make good on any threat.

"If there's only two, they can't cover all the elevators and stairs. If we get a chance to see just one, I'll take him out and grab his weapon. That'll even the odds somewhat. The intention is to take the stairs down as far as we can go. You ready?" He turned and looked at both of them. When he got a nod from each, he opened the door to the hall wider and slipped out. Quietly he motioned to the stairwell to the left. He raced toward it and pushed open the door. They were right behind him.

No sound came from below. He was taking a risk, but

they had very few options. Moving as silently as they could, the three made it down one set of stairs. Still nobody. Rather than trying for an elevator, considering that Sienna was still strong enough to keep going down the other three flights, he moved them forward, and on they went down to the third, the second, and the first.

Something inside him said it was way too damn easy. At the main floor, he paused and looked through the glass window in the door, where he saw one of the security guards holding a weapon on the rest, who would normally be the last to leave after completing a full sweep of the building.

Shit. This was an inside job. Robert caught a glance at what was outside the window too. His gaze widened, and he shook his head. Rhodes immediately placed his finger to his lips and motioned them to continue down to the parking garage level. They had to get somewhere they could hide.

At least in the garage there would be vehicles. There was only one more floor. He was careful as he peered through the door window. He couldn't see anybody. Taking a chance, he pulled it ajar slightly. No alarms went off.

He pulled it fully open and motioned the other two out ahead of him. They immediately raced to the first vehicle and crouched down beside it. He didn't see anyone standing guard, so he joined them. He didn't know how the underground system here worked, but there must be some kind of an open gate to enter and exit through. But they had to get there first. In the background, he heard something that made his blood chill.

"Did that door just open?" someone yelled too damn close by.

From the opposite side, on his right, came the answer.

"I didn't see anybody come out."

From the left again came someone speaking. "You're supposed to stand there, keeping an eye out, making sure nobody escaped."

"I was, remember? Then he sent me over to check out the ramp. Make sure nobody walked in or out." The man's voice was frustrated. "I can't watch everything. What the hell are you doing?"

There was only silence to Rhodes's left.

And Rhodes knew the man was on the move. He motioned for the others to stay low against the vehicle. He peered around the back of the car, his ear cocked, listening hard. He could hear footsteps approaching. Desperate to keep the gunman away from Sienna and Robert, he raced around the car to intercept him.

"What the—"

One solid blow to the throat and the gunman crumpled to his knees. Rhodes caught him as he pitched forward and slowly lowered the man to the ground. Rhodes pulled the semiautomatic weapon off his shoulder and slipped it over his own.

He crept forward to the front of the car and around to squat quietly beside Robert and Sienna.

"Hey, Jimmy, is that you?"

Damn. Rhodes had hoped for a minute's window before the other guy realized his buddy was not answering. Still, Rhodes had a weapon now.

At the sound of running footsteps, he huddled at the front of the vehicle and waited. If he could take out both these assholes, that would give the SWAT team a chance to come in. They needed a clear entrance into the building.

He could see Robert had his phone out, sending a text, alerting the police probably. That was all fine and dandy, but

Rhodes wanted these two out of here before the bloodshed started.

"Jimmy?"

Silence.

Rhodes's muscles tensed as he waited. The second gunman's footsteps slowed, and Rhodes heard the shifting of the weapon in his hands. But he no longer called for his friend. Rhodes heard the gunman's footsteps coming closer, and he counted them off in his head. Three. Two. One. He stood up and fired. One single shot. The second gunman dropped, his weapon banging to the ground.

Rhodes raced over and kicked the second weapon free. One bullet to the upper shoulder, but he was unconscious and bleeding heavily. He dragged the gunman over to join his buddy, then went back and picked up the second weapon. Using his shoulder as a harness, he threw it over his back and went around to Robert and Sienna.

"That's the two who were on guard down here," he said. "Come on. We'll head toward the ramp. With them down, that leaves law enforcement an avenue to get in."

He ushered them quickly through the rows of parked vehicles to the exit. Up ahead he could see one single bar across the road. At least there was no floor-to-ceiling gate at the entrance. They should be able to get out without any trouble.

He pulled them back just as they were about to walk up. "We have to be careful, in case a sniper is out there."

They both froze.

Sienna looked at him. "Is that likely?"

He shot her a look and said, "Would you have thought this building would've been taken over by gunmen? Was that likely?"

Robert made a single call. "We're free down in the parking garage. We've taken out two gunmen watching this
entrance. We're standing by the ramp. Not sure if there's any
snipers to stop our escape. Vehicles can come in here. It's
clear." And he hung up.

Two minutes later a SWAT vehicle came ripping
through to the underground parking level. Several men
jumped out and raced toward them, weapons raised. Rhodes
held up his hands. Robert stepped forward and quickly
explained.

As much as he didn't want to, because they still weren't
free and clear, Rhodes quickly gave up the confiscated
weapons. They were ushered as a group outside to the street
level. There they were quickly moved around to the corner of
the block where the police had a control center set up.

Sienna clung to Rhodes's side. They were quickly
checked over, and when he turned around, Robert was gone.

Realizing the SWAT focus would be on the building, he
pulled Sienna farther back out of the way and said, "Feel like
sneaking off and getting out of here?"

She looked up at him gratefully. "Can we?" She pointed
at the front of the building. "Isn't that where you parked?"

He stared over at the vehicle, then at the surrounding
chaos. He made a fast decision. "Stay here."

And he bolted for the truck.

Chapter 11

S HE WANTED TO call him back but knew it would be useless. He was already on the move. Besides, they needed the wheels. But she wasn't sure the law enforcement officers would let him grab the vehicle and go. They were likely to shoot him first and ask questions later. At times like this, it was just crazy out there.

Still, acting like a man who knew exactly what he was doing, he walked over and unlocked the truck, got in, started it up, pulled it forward and around the corner. Several policemen converged on him at that point. When he quickly explained who he was, they allowed him to pass. He pulled up beside her and opened the window. "Get in."

She didn't need a second urging. She raced around to the far side, opened the passenger door and got in. They were moving before she got the seat belt buckled. "Should we tell anyone we're going?"

"Send a text to Levi and tell him to inform Robert we're leaving. Or better yet"—he pulled out his phone and tossed it toward her—"find Robert's number under the contacts and send him a text."

She did as he said. The response came in very quickly. "He says, **Thanks for the update. And a bigger one for the rescue. I owe you.**" She laughed. "There's a lot worse things than having the DA owe you a favor."

She glanced around as he drove the small truck through the city streets. "Should we stay and give a statement?"

"Do you want to? I thought you wanted to get home."

"I want to get home and stay there," she corrected. "If we have to come back to give one, then there's no point in leaving just now." She sat there in frustration. "But then, this might not be settled for hours yet." She glanced at the time and added, "It's almost six o'clock. And we've already been there once today."

"We can go to the police station and do something about it right now if you want."

"It's an option."

She could see him wavering. Sure enough he turned the corner and then several more.

They pulled up outside the station. "Let's go in and take care of our citizens' duty," he said calmly. "After that, we're either grabbing dinner and a hotel, or we're going home. You decide."

Only it wasn't that easy. By the time they walked in and talked to someone, and that person realized they were actually in the building, part of the mess going on downtown, they were quickly ushered into a room and told to wait. Several people came in and asked questions; proof of identity was handed over. And then finally the same man they had spoken to earlier walked in and sat down.

"Rhodes, it's good to see you again." He reached over and shook hands. He turned his gaze to Sienna. "Now, young lady, why is it that you were likely to be one of the targets all over again?"

She glanced at Rhodes and then back to the big man. "Same reason as last time. I was helping the DA gather information for a case. Only I was kidnapped and just released from the hospital. We dropped off the DA's laptop I'd been working on. That's when we found out the building was taken over."

"You've just had a shitty day then, haven't you?"

She laughed. "That's one way to look at it." After that, she was asked a series of questions. She gave the details she could remember. Several times she just said, "You will have to ask the DA about that."

When she finally answered all his questions, he turned his attention to Rhodes. "Now, as I understand it, you have a very different take of what was going on. Let's go through it from the top."

Sienna collapsed back into her chair, tuning out most of the conversation going on around her. After all the questions, it was like the stuffing had been ripped out of her. She should've just stayed in the hospital. At least there she would be resting right now. She was feeling woozy again.

All she wanted to do was sleep. With her head pounding, body aching a whole lot more, she realized a hotel might be the better answer for tonight. It also looked like they weren't getting there any time soon. She glanced down at her watch and saw it was well past eight and she groaned.

She closed her eyes. Tried to silence her thoughts.

"We're leaving, now." Rhodes stood up. "She was only released from the hospital just before three and got involved in that downtown mess within the hour," he said to the detective. "I'll take her to a hotel, get her some food. She needs to lie down."

The detective stood up. "Please stay close. I don't know how quickly we'll get downtown wrapped up, but we'll probably have more questions for you. And I understand that your home is a few hours away. You don't want to come all the way back here to do this again." He glanced at Sienna, who was now shaky but standing valiantly and holding on to the table. "You need to rest."

She gave a half laugh. "I believe I have been trying to do that since I left the hospital."

Rhodes walked over and wrapped his arm around her shoulders. "If you have a card, I'll call you from whichever hotel we're at."

The detective immediately pulled one out of his wallet and handed it to him. "Just send me a text. Let's make sure you guys don't disappear off the grid for a third time."

Sienna stared at him in shock. "Please don't even joke about that." She moved toward the door, but it was suddenly looking very far away. Even with Rhodes's arm around her shoulders, she felt the room spin. "I ..." she muttered. She stopped and grabbed the chair for support. She glanced over at Rhodes. "I'm sorry."

She registered his stare of surprise as her knees sagged.

He quickly swung her up in his arms and said, "That's it. Back to the hospital."

With the last of her strength she whispered, "No. No hospital. Just a hotel. Just let me have a bed so I can lie down."

WITH THE DETECTIVE walking alongside him, holding open the doors out to his truck, Rhodes carried Sienna carefully in his arms. "You sure you don't want to be taken to the hospital?"

The detective used Rhodes's keys and unlocked the door. "Head wounds are tricky."

Rhodes said, "Unfortunately, I know that all too well."

He carefully placed her in the seat and buckled her in. He turned and thanked the detective, accepting his keys back. He shut the passenger door and walked around to the driver's side. "I need a place where I can carry her into the room without raising alarms. Any ideas?"

"Several motels about four miles down the road. On the right."

"Good enough."

Rhodes hopped in and turned on the engine. Checking traffic, he pulled out and kept going down the same street. It was getting late, so darkness was falling. He didn't want to be anywhere close to the mess downtown. By now they should have all the gunmen secured, but he wouldn't count on it. Often they would just hold off, wait and see what the gunmen did. It depended whether they had a whole parcel of hostages or not. They didn't have Sienna or Robert now, and for that, he was glad for the decision to pull out.

Life didn't always work out that way.

There were several motels, just as the detective had described. Rhodes pulled into the parking lot of one and went to turn off the engine, but instinct prodded him.

What were the chances somebody might have overheard or that the detective wasn't on the up-and-up? Suspicious by nature, he couldn't quite leave it alone.

He pulled back out onto the main road and found another motel on the opposite side, about two blocks down. He pulled into that one. Leaving Sienna locked inside the vehicle, he walked in and booked a room on the main floor. With the key and receipt in hand, he drove around to the far side and parked outside the room with the coordinating number on the key.

"This is good," he muttered under his breath. "Now for

Sienna."

He got out of the truck and unlocked the room, then returned to carefully unbuckle her. He lifted her in his arms and carried her into the hotel room, laying her down on top of the king-size bed. There hadn't been any twin beds on the main floor, and he wanted to exit fast if they needed to. So one bed was what they had to share. With the shape she was in, she just needed to be comfortable.

Another trip out, and he brought in their luggage and the picnic basket. He quickly locked the truck and then the hotel door behind him. They needed food, or at least he did. She needed to sleep for as long as she could. But when she woke, she would be starving. There was still some of the traveling food from Alfred. But it was looking less than prime.

He opened the night table drawers for any brochures of fast food places close by. A pizza shop was across the street. If need be, he could make a quick phone call and have that delivered. He didn't care how close the place was, he wasn't leaving Sienna's side again tonight.

Chapter 12

S HE WOKE UP several times in the night, and each time she felt a strong hand reach out and stroke her arm. At one point, her arm was tucked under the covers, and the blanket pulled up to her neck. He still managed to find it with a reassuring pat.

"Just sleep. You're safe."

Realizing Rhodes was on watch, she tumbled back under.

When she woke the next morning, instead of feeling refreshed and wide awake, her body was heavy, resisting movement of any kind. It was the first full sleep she'd had since the kidnapping. And therefore, it was actually the day after the event, and everything hurt. She had to go to the bathroom in a big way, but just the thought of standing, let alone walking that far, made the throbbing pound even heavier and harder.

She rolled over slightly to see Rhodes sleeping atop the covers beside her. He was still fully dressed, in warrior mode just in case. A sleeping giant. But all alpha when awake. And she had to admit—she loved that. She lay there as long as she could before her need grew too intense to ignore.

She eased back the covers, slipped out from underneath them and straightened. She caught her breath, but she managed to get to the bathroom. She wished she had something for the pain. She didn't really want to take anything chemical, but holy crap, she hurt. After she used the bathroom, she eyed the shower and wondered. She wasn't sure she could stand long enough for that, but a soak would be lovely. She glanced back into the room to see Rhodes still napping.

Decision made, she filled the bathtub with hot water. Stripping off her clothes, she sank into the warm heat. And that's when she realized she had more than just bangs, bumps, and bruises. There were several scrapes. They stung as she eased into the tub, and it took several moments of biting her lip until she felt she would not cry out. Finally, she lay there totally submerged—the warmth washing over her, easing deep into her sore muscles. This was more like it. She hoped this would give her flexibility to move easier.

Using the soap available, she did a quick shampoo and rinse, being careful with her head wound. Dried blood remained in her hair, but she did her best to get most of it. She soaked as long as she thought she could, then pulled the plug. She stood, still a little wobbly, and grabbed a towel. Dry and wrapped up, she headed back into the main room. It didn't look like Rhodes had moved at all. She was sorry he'd had such a poor night looking after her. A good night's sleep was so necessary for healing.

Taking her bag off to the side, she lifted it onto a chair and selected some clean clothes. She managed to pull on her underwear and then dropped her towel and quickly dressed.

It was light outside, and she was very hungry. She walked back into the bathroom and hung up her towel. While in there, she brushed her teeth, and feeling ready to start the day, returned to the room and found Rhodes sitting up in bed, looking as alert as she'd ever seen him.

"I'm sorry. I hope I didn't wake you."

He bounced to his feet and said, "I've been awake. Just dozing off and on." He checked his watch, opened his phone and made a quick call.

Realizing it was business as usual, and hopeful maybe they could go home, she quickly repacked her bag and sat down on the bed to wait for him.

When he was done, he turned to her. "Robert wants to know if we can meet for breakfast."

"I presume you said yes"—she nodded at the phone in his hand—"especially as the phone call is already finished."

He laughed and took her gently in his arms. "I figured you didn't want to meet him. But if we have to eat breakfast anyway, might as well combine the two." He studied her critically, then kissed her gently on her temple. "You obviously had a good night. You're looking so much better."

"You are definitely right about not wanting to meet him. But if we can meet, eat, and then leave …" She smiled. "It's the best of both worlds." She stopped and said, "I'm starved."

He shook his head as he reached for her bag. "You're just rushing me along so we can get to the food faster."

She grinned. He loaded the luggage in the truck, came back and went into the washroom. When he returned, he stopped in the doorway. "Ready?"

She nodded. "Absolutely."

They were fifteen minutes away from the restaurant where they had arranged to meet. As they walked in, they found Robert already in a booth by the window. He waved at them, and they sat down on the same side, facing him.

"Good morning, Sienna," Robert said in a low voice. "You're looking much better."

"Then it's a facade," she said with a half laugh. "I woke up this morning to find I had more muscles than I ever remembered feeling before, and every one was screaming."

He nodded in commiseration. "You went through a lot yesterday. Take several days off just to rest and relax."

"That's all I plan to do for the next three days. I'm hoping to go home and crash on my bed and just do nothing."

Robert turned his attention to Rhodes. "I wanted to thank you personally for getting me out of there yesterday." He nodded toward Sienna. "For getting us both out."

"Not an issue. I did what I could." Rhodes laced his fingers on the table in front of him. "How did the armed gunmen situation downtown end?"

"Unfortunately, all six are dead."

"Six?" Sienna shook her head. "I thought there were only two."

"Two on the garage level," Rhodes clarified. He turned to gaze back at Robert.

"Actually, four were in the main building. Plus, the two we encountered on the garage level."

"I didn't kill the men in the garage. I only knocked out one and shot the other in the shoulder."

"Then somebody came along and put a bullet in both their heads," Robert said.

Rhodes sat back. "Which means there was a seventh."

Robert nodded. "That's what we're thinking."

"Wouldn't that be too obvious?" Sienna asked. "Why would he have done that?"

"Dead men don't talk." Rhodes reached over and covered her hands with his.

She sighed and gently unlocked her hands from the fists they'd become and held on to his instead.

Just then a waitress walked by, holding a full pot of coffee. "May I offer you some?" she asked with a smile.

Gratefully, they pushed their cups toward her so she could fill them up.

When done, she motioned at the menus in front of them. "Are you ready to order breakfast?"

"Absolutely." Sienna hadn't even looked at the menu. "I'm starving."

"If you'd like our special, it's a big breakfast. Three eggs, sausage, bacon, ham, pancakes, hash browns, and toast."

"Sounds fantastic. I'll have that." She'd ordered a ton of carbs, but with her energy level right now, that was just what she needed.

"Make that two," Rhodes said. They handed the unopened menus back to the waitress as Robert ordered just coffee.

Feeling much better with coffee in her hand, a meal ordered and Rhodes at her side, Sienna sat back to wait. She just didn't know what she was waiting for.

SO THIS WASN'T just a social call, allowing Robert a chance to give thanks. Not that Rhodes wanted or needed any. And it wasn't exactly doing his job, but if he could help, then he would. He'd been capable of so much more, but he couldn't leave Sienna alone. She'd been through enough already. They'd gotten lucky. He knew that. That didn't mean he would be so lucky at the next encounter. And there would be one with the seventh man still free.

Had the killer seen them? Had he been in the garage level while they'd been there? If so, would he let them just walk away, somehow knowing they hadn't seen him?

DALE MAYER

He glanced at Sienna. If he brought it up, it was just one more thing for her to worry about. That wasn't exactly what he wanted. But sticking their heads in the sand wasn't an answer either.

Sienna stared right back at him. "Are you going to say it or am I?"

He raised one eyebrow at her.

She looked at Robert. "Chances are very good whoever killed the men in the garage to silence them also knows we escaped. I'm pretty sure his plan is that we don't live to talk about it either."

Instead of answering, Rhodes squeezed her fingers gently. He glanced back at Robert to see him staring at the two of them in surprise.

"Were there any surviving hostages?" Rhodes asked.

"Yes. Our security people all lived through this. Thankfully, the other employees and visitors left the building early on." He glanced back to Sienna. "As you see, the six gunmen didn't shoot anyone." Rhodes laughed. "So there's a good chance nobody's after us at all." But even he didn't sound convinced.

Sierra gave a half snort. "And if you believe that, I've got a bridge I want to sell you."

Rhodes didn't mention the two dead bodies he and Merk had found in the empty house that could possibly be somehow involved too. Probably killed by one or two of the dead gunmen. Just because they didn't kill anybody in the downtown Dallas hostage situation doesn't mean they haven't killed people elsewhere. "The seventh man could have seen all three of us together in the garage," Rhodes said calmly. He turned to look at Robert.

"It would be easy enough to see I was meeting with

you," Sienna snapped. Then she calmed down. "Look, I don't want this guy to come after me, but I'm not exactly comfortable thinking he'll forget about us either."

"He still would have to know who you are," Robert said. "Your names were kept out of the news release."

"Right." After that she didn't say anything else; just sat quietly.

Rhodes glanced back at Robert and said, "Are you planning on staying around? Do you have a bodyguard? Do you have a security detail just in case?"

"Actually, I ran that by the department, but they think the chance of this guy coming after me is pretty low."

"Of course they do. No budget money, I presume."

He nodded. "I see you're familiar with that department line."

The waitress returned with hefty platters of food, then refilled Robert's coffee cup. "I'll be back in a few minutes with your toast."

And she disappeared.

Sienna let the conversation drift around her as she began eating the food.

Rhodes was slower, taking his time. He contemplated how much danger they were actually in. The killer would likely already know who they were, and if not, it wouldn't be hard to find out. But Robert was more likely to be in danger.

The waitress returned with their toast and they nodded their thanks. They quietly ate for several long minutes.

"Do you have the identities of the dead gunmen?" Rhodes asked. "I'm presuming it's got something to do with the case Sienna was helping you with?"

"When I left last night, they were working on that. I haven't seen or heard the names yet. I can forward them to you when I do."

"That would be helpful. At least I can check them off my wanted list," Rhodes said drily. "Plus, it may lead us to the seventh man. What about the laptop being bugged?"

Robert shook his head. "According to Bobby, they couldn't find anything on it. Are you sure your results were right?"

Rhodes shrugged. "No. But are you sure no one in your office took the sheets out of the ledger? Same person could be bugging the equipment in your office."

"We'll open an investigation into the department, but as much as I could hope for answers, I doubt they'll come fast." He then gave them a sober smile. "We're on it."

That lightened the mood, and they finished the rest of the meal with other conversation. As he got up to leave, Robert collected the check and said, "I would like to have you come back to the office and give us a hand with this case, but I understand the need to go home and rest."

They shook hands, and then Rhodes led Sienna out to the truck. He stopped outside the restaurant to look around the area. He could sense nothing wrong.

In a way this was a whole new day. Sienna stepped up beside him, slipping her hand into his and said, "Are we good to go?"

"Yes, we are."

Chapter 13

S HE WANTED TO laugh and crow in delight as Rhodes finally pulled the truck into traffic and took the turn toward home. At the same time she didn't trust it. It was hard not to keep looking behind them to see if they were being followed. So she continued checking the side mirror on her side. But the farther they went, the more she relaxed. After they'd traveled for more than an hour, Rhodes turned to her and said, "Go ahead and have a nap if you want."

She shook her head. "Actually, I slept decently last night." She studied his face and said, "You're the one who didn't."

"I slept enough," he said. "This is an easy drive home."

"Good thing. I'm more than ready to be back there. I hope we don't have to return for court or anything else."

"There's no point. All those men are dead, and we've already given our statements."

"Do you think the killer will come after us, making sure nobody can talk?"

"Anything's possible." He glanced down at the fuel gauge. "We need some gas. I'll turn off at the next stop I see. But there has to be much more at stake to kill all his men. The DA will sort this out."

She nodded. Her bladder needed to be emptied again also. She'd had so much coffee at breakfast, she probably wouldn't need any more until tomorrow morning. Still, the comforting drink would be nice for the rest of the trip.

Up ahead was an off-ramp that headed to a truck stop. Rhodes quickly took the turn, and after driving around, he pulled up to a gas pump and turned off the engine.

She hopped out. "I'm going to find the ladies' room."

He nodded, busy putting his credit card into the machine, grabbing the pump.

She walked into the restaurant area and followed the signs to the washrooms. She was done a few minutes later but took the opportunity to brush her hair and wash her face again. Just being in the truck for that long was making her tired. She didn't want to sleep anymore.

She walked back outside to see Rhodes still filling up the truck and called over, "You want a coffee?"

"Sure."

She turned back into the restaurant and ordered two, and since they had fresh muffins on the counter, she picked up an assortment. They certainly wouldn't stop for another meal after that big breakfast, but having a muffin, you could never go wrong.

After paying for the food, she carried the tray of coffees and bag of muffins out to the truck. Several vehicles were leaving the parking lot, so she had to dodge them before she could cross to the truck. She stowed the cups inside where they were safe and secure. She saw no sign of Rhodes.

She closed the passenger door and walked around to the side. Rhodes had collapsed on the ground, his arms stretched above his head. She dropped to his side, crying out, "Rhodes, what happened?"

But he didn't answer. She shook him gently. He groaned and then opened his eyes to stare at her. Awareness filled his gaze. "Somebody hit me from behind," he said. "I was just putting the pump back, and somebody reached out with a pipe or something and smashed me in the head. I went down, but I don't think I lost consciousness." He slowly sat up.

"Did you see who it was?" she asked, hating to think they'd been followed this far. She bounded to her feet and turned to see if anybody was still around. But of course, they weren't. They would've taken off immediately. She'd seen dozens of vehicles leave.

As she looked back down at him, she found Rhodes standing again, holding on to the side of the truck for stability. Instantly, she wrapped her arms around him to help. He turned and leaned against the side panel, taking several deep breaths, his arm holding her close. "I didn't expect that."

"Neither of us did." She glanced around again, wondering if she should call for help, then realized that was foolish. She faced him. "You want to call the police?"

He snorted. "Hell, no. But you're driving." He pulled the keys from his pocket and handed them to her. Then he slowly, using the truck bed for support, walked around to the passenger side. After making sure he was settled, she opened the driver's side and hopped in, turning on the engine. "I have no problem getting us home," she said, "but I'm worried about your head."

"Don't worry about that. I'm pretty tough—hard to crack."

"Yeah, but the headache that comes afterward will just about kill you." She carefully drove out and took the ramp leading them back onto the main freeway. "You might as well relax and rest," she said. "We've got a couple hours to go." She couldn't stop herself from looking over at him in worry. "But please don't sleep. You're never supposed to after a head injury."

He shot her a look and said, "I won't, nor will I pass out. But until my blurry vision restabilizes, I'm not the one to be driving."

She winced at the thought. "How about you try to text Levi and tell him what happened. No way in hell this was an accident."

"Well, if it was deliberate, they did a poor job," he said, "because they left me alive, and that's always a mistake."

"Maybe they didn't have the right man."

"More than likely too many people were around, so he couldn't get you at that time." He pulled out his phone and sent off several texts, starting a flow of discussions as his phone buzzed and beeped multiple times during the next fifteen minutes. That was good. She wanted the whole damn team involved in this. Somebody had attacked one of their own, and that couldn't be allowed to happen.

She would get him home to the rest of the team so they could all help. This was so far beyond her. She didn't do trouble. She'd told them that already.

Driving carefully, she kept the truck moving steadily toward home. The last thing she wanted was another incident. But thankfully it was a straight and quiet drive—too quiet. She kept checking on Rhodes, but he looked awful, collapsed against the passenger door. By the time she took the turnoff and drove past the small town close to the compound, she could feel the tension keeping her body rigid. She was so damn sore now it was nearly impossible to drive. A headache was starting again, but as she glanced over at Rhodes, leaning back with his eyes closed, she knew she was better off than he was. As she pulled into the compound and parked, turning off the engine, she muttered, "Instead of the returning heroes, we're a sorry pair."

"We're fine. We survived. That's what we do."

She turned sideways to look at him. She was aware of the others coming out of the compound, racing toward them. "Is that really the bottom line here?"

He reached up with a hand and gently stroked her cheek. "There's no way I'd let anything happen to you," he whispered. "You'll be fine."

"Is that what you think this is all about?" She shook her head. "You're a fool."

"I promised your brother I'd look after you," he said, opening his door.

She froze. "I make those decisions myself. I understand wanting to keep an eye out to make sure I don't get hurt unnecessarily, but don't you dare sacrifice yourself to save me."

She opened her door and hopped out, finding Ice standing there. Her intense gaze searched Sienna from top to bottom.

"We'll unload the truck," Ice ordered. "You get your ass up to bed."

Sienna gave her a wan smile. "And here I thought I looked pretty good."

Ice snorted. "Move it."

"Only if you insist Rhodes goes to."

Ice gave a clipped nod. "That's exactly what'll happen."

Hoping Ice was serious and not willing to argue anymore, Sienna made her way to her suite. She sat on the bed, kicking off her shoes, when Levi came up, carrying her bags. Stopping in the doorway, he dropped them to the side, looking at her. "Will you be okay here alone?"

"I'll be fine," she whispered. "The drive back was pretty nerve-wracking. I kept worrying he was hurt more seriously than he was letting on."

"That's Rhodes. Hell, it's any of us in that same situation. We hate to be injured in the first place. We never admit to it being as bad as it is."

She stretched out on her bed and moaned as her head sank into the pillow. "You'd better check him over then because, as far as he's concerned, it's nothing. But I believe he was out cold for a few minutes."

"Will do." And he closed the door gently behind him.

That's the last thing she remembered as she closed her eyes and let the world disappear.

RHODES SAT DOWN at the kitchen table. As much as he wanted to crash, that wouldn't happen soon. A slew of communications continued since he'd arrived home. And he was feeling relatively fine. Not that Ice listened to him. She checked his head wound and clucked like a mother hen. Something he'd never heard from her before.

"You sure you didn't see anything?"

"You should ask Sienna that. She came around with coffees right after I hit the ground." He raised his gaze to look at Levi. "She might've seen the vehicle as it drove off."

"According to her, you were actually unconscious for a few moments," Levi said.

Rhodes frowned. "I don't think so. I could still hear the vehicles driving past."

"Any chance it was a punk just looking to steal your wallet?" Stone asked from Rhodes's side.

Rhodes shrugged. "You know how I feel about coincidence…"

"The same way we all do," Stone interrupted. "She's kidnapped. You both get caught up in a hostage situation. You take out two men in your bid to escape, and both are found with a bullet to the head, execution style, and the next morning you're attacked at a gas station as you leave town." Stone shook his head. "Sloppy."

"Exactly. And now we know for sure someone is after us. I did warn Robert that somebody would likely come after him, as it had been well-reported in the news how he had escaped the attack on the building. His office in particular."

"So somebody knew you two were there as well?"

"Anything's possible. SWAT and dozens of cops were around. Honestly, I didn't see anybody suspicious, but people could've talked, or placed bugs in the conference room or DA's office. Several of the hostages were released afterward. Maybe one of them said something. There should be cameras in the parking level."

"They were shot at," Ice said. "We'll find out."

As the conversation dwindled, Rhodes looked around at the rest of them. "If you guys don't mind, I'm going to crash." He stood up and walked to the doorway, his hand instinctively reaching out to grab on the frame. The room was circling around him.

He could hear the cries behind him. The next thing he knew, Stone had his arm wrapped around Rhodes's rib cage, supporting him.

"Easy does it, buddy. Let me give you a hand."

Muttering his thanks, and using Stone for support, they got into the elevator and went to the second floor. There Stone helped Rhodes into his suite. He made the last few

DALE MAYER

steps to the bed and sank down into the waiting softness. He kicked off his shoes and stretched out, then said, "Turn out the light, will you? It's killing my eyes."

Instantly the room darkened. Stone stood at the open doorway, and Rhodes knew what the problem was. "I'll be fine. Come back and check on me in an hour if you want. I just need to rest." He rolled over to his side, punched the pillow under his head and closed his eyes.

He vaguely heard Stone's heavy footsteps as he walked away while hushed voices remained outside in the hall. That was fine with him. His friends had his back.

Chapter 14

SIENNA WOKE TO talking in the hallway. She froze, terror turning her blood cold until she identified Levi and Ice's very distinctive voices. She had yet to recognize everybody by just hearing them speak.

"He's still sleeping."

"Was he responding when you spoke to him?" Ice asked, the concern in her voice evident.

It took Sienna a few minutes to figure out they were talking about Rhodes. She sat up slowly, slipped on her shoes and walked out to the hallway. "How is he?"

Ice spun around, walked over immediately, her hand capturing Sienna's. "How are you feeling?"

Sienna smiled. "The sleep did me good. I feel much better. I'm worried about Rhodes. Should I have taken him to the hospital?" She clung to Ice's hand. "He was pretty resistant to the idea of going anywhere but home. I suggested we call the police, but he didn't like that either."

"No, there was no point in this instance," Ice said. "He's got a concussion, so we just wanted to keep an eye on him."

"Is somebody standing watch over him all the time?" Sienna frowned as she walked toward his door. She knew Rhodes slept solid. "I'd like to stay with him if that's possible." She turned to look at Ice.

"We're all checking on him pretty closely. Nobody needs

to be here full time." As if seeing something in Sienna's face, Ice rushed to say, "If you want to stay for a while, that'd be okay. You can let me know if his condition changes."

Sienna nodded. "I'll do that." She looked around and said, "I'll grab my laptop and a cup of coffee then sit with him for a while."

"I'm heading to the kitchen, so I'll bring you a cup. Get your laptop or whatever you need. I'll meet you back here." Ice turned and left with Levi.

Sienna returned to her suite, right next door, grabbed her sweater to ward off the chill she still felt and pulled out her laptop. She wasn't useless here. Robert was supposed to send the names of the men who had been killed in the hostage situation. And right now she really wanted to know if those names matched up with any of the ones she'd found. She grabbed a power charger and headed over to Rhodes's suite.

It took a lot of effort, but she moved the big chair closer to the bed so she could sit down and put her feet up, then she plugged in the laptop and turned it on. When Ice came in, Sienna was already researching the news articles to see what coverage there had been regarding the attack on the DA's office.

She smiled up at Ice and said, "Thank you." She nodded at her laptop. "Did Robert send you the names of the dead gunmen?"

"I believe he sent them to Levi." Ice put the cup of coffee on the night table beside Rhodes's bed. In a low voice she whispered, "Why?"

"I want to check their names against the spreadsheets."

"Good idea. I'll email them to you." With one last glance at the two of them, she backed out of the bedroom, disappearing around the corner.

Sienna opened her email program, and within minutes she had an incoming one from Ice. Sienna clicked on it, bringing up the names. She glanced through them, but they meant nothing to her. She popped each name separately into Google to see what kind of history would come up. Then she copied them over to her notes on the case and searched the spreadsheets she'd created.

And came up with nothing.

Damn it. She'd been so sure something was here. Some way she could make sense of all this.

So far she drew a blank. But she wasn't ready to give up.

An hour later she wasn't getting anywhere. Except tired. She closed the laptop, slipped down in the chair and closed her eyes.

A gentle touch on her foot woke her up a few minutes later. She glanced over at the bed to see Rhodes there, a smile on his face, his hand around her foot. She gave him a lazy grin and asked, "Is this how you spend your days, just lazing about in bed?"

"Well, I would if you joined me," he said lightly. "That sounds like fun."

He stroked her calf. But she didn't want to let him know how his words affected her. She gave him a light sneer and said, "You think too much of yourself if you believe you can keep it up for days."

With a glint in his eyes he turned his gaze to hers. "Is that a challenge?"

She laughed. "It so isn't."

He propped himself up on his bed, his fingers lightly drawing a pattern on her foot, around her ankle and slowly up her calf. "Anytime you want, ... sweetheart."

"Yeah, what about Jarrod?" she reminded him. Her gaze was sharp as she studied his face, looking for any sign of change.

But there was none. Jarrod's name didn't appear to make any difference to Rhodes.

"If and when we have a relationship, your brother will accept it," he said. "Trust me."

She opened her eyes wide and stared at him again. "Okay, if you say so." She dropped her feet to the floor and stood up. "I'll let the others know you're awake." She grabbed her coffee cup.

As she went to step through the door, he called back. "Wait."

She turned around to face him, one eyebrow raised. "What do you need?"

"You."

His voice was so low and soft she almost didn't hear it. Frowning, her eyes searching his, she walked back into the room and sat down beside him on the bed. "What did you say?"

"You heard me."

She continued to study his face, but his gaze was clear, with a glint of humor, but also something else. Sincerity? Passion? She reached up to stroke his cheek, her thumb drifting down to gently follow the curve of his lips.

He grabbed her hand, held it to his lips and kissed it. Then he tugged her slowly toward him. When her head was just above his, his hand slipped up to the back of her neck and he pulled her all the way down and kissed her.

"Yes, I mean that." When he finally released her, he whispered, "We've been dancing around this for weeks. I figured one of us had to make that move to cross the divide."

Still dazed from the touch of his lips and the heat coursing through her system, she asked in confusion, "Divide?"

"Your brother. You seem to think he'll have a problem if we have a relationship."

"I figured you thought that," she corrected him, her breath catching in the back of her throat, but that look in his eyes, ... she was drowning ...

He flashed a wicked grin her way and said, "I might have, but I already spoke to him about us."

She gasped. "You what? Why?"

"So we'd have this out of the way. Because he warned me off when I first met you. I had to let him know I couldn't follow that dictate now. You matter too much. He knew it already—we just needed to clear the air."

She studied him carefully. "So what does that mean now?" she teased. "Do we go for coffee dates? Or are you looking for something else?"

"I'm not looking for anything," he said. "I've already found something special. I guess I want to see where we take it."

He reached up and captured her cheek. With his thumb running across her lips, he tugged her down a little bit more as he rose up on his elbow and kissed her again. "Why don't we try? Why not give us a chance? That same chance we've always wanted to be given." In a voice dark with passion, he dropped kisses on her chin, cheeks, and eyebrows. "Say yes," he whispered. "To this. ... To us. ... To right now."

It was what she'd wanted. All she had wanted. She leaned closer and kissed him ever-so-gently and whispered, "Yes."

He pulled her down to the bed with him. She let out a startled cry.

Rolling her over flat on the bed, his body covered hers, and his lips crushed hers. She had only nanoseconds to understand how quickly their positions had changed. The insistent prodding against her pelvis had her blood pulsing though her body; liquid pooled between her legs.

Dear God, she wanted him. She just hadn't expected this right now. They'd spent two nights in a hotel already, and now they were home, and she was wrapped in his arms in his bed. Just where she wanted to be.

It wasn't that it was bad timing but … She wrenched her mouth free and whispered, "The door."

Rhodes stared down at her in confusion, already with passion clouding his vision. He glanced at the open door, back at her, and was up off the bed, walking toward it.

She laughed and watched as he stuck his head out in the hallway, then closed the door and locked it. As he turned to face her, she scrambled to her knees and waited for him to come to her.

Only he didn't. He stopped in the middle of the room as if to give her a chance to change her mind.

He opened his mouth to say something and then closed it. And she understood. It wasn't that he was uncertain, but he was unsure about her. She gave him a slow dawning smile of passion and heat. She grabbed the corners of her T-shirt and pulled it over her head, dropping it to the side. Then she stood on the bed and took off her jeans. Standing before him, long and lean, in just her panties and bra, she waited to see what he'd do.

He caught his breath, then galvanized into action. He stripped right down to his skin.

Slowly he walked toward her, his erection standing proud. She dropped to her knees, her legs suddenly too weak to hold her.

He swept her in his arms before she could lie down again and tugged her close. Hot flesh seared and stoked the fire within. Brushing his lips against hers, he whispered, "You're still wearing too much."

Her lips tilted into a smile as she kissed him back. "I think you can take care of that." And she kissed him passionately, pouring out all the loss, loneliness, and desire she had kept reined in for the last couple months.

She had tossed and turned at night, deciding whether to stay, because of him, or if she wanted to be a part of this whole unit. That he was here was definitely a plus. If he wouldn't be hers, then it would be hard. And if he had other women, it would be damn-near impossible. It wasn't what she wanted for her life, for herself.

But this was absolutely what she wanted. Cool air swept between their heated bodies as he stepped back to drop her bra onto the floor. Instantly she was crushed against his chest, the cool skin of her breasts pressing hard against his muscled chest. She stroked and caressed, her fingers frantic as they explored.

"Slowly," he whispered. "We have lots of time."

She slid her hands up to grab his face and study the look in his eyes. "You don't think they'll come looking for you?"

"They'll come. They'll see the closed door. They'll assume I'm in the shower, or we're busy."

She winced.

"Don't worry about it. They already know."

Her lips twitched. "And here I thought I'd kept the secret to myself."

"Yeah. I've been teased about it already several times." He slid his hand down to her butt and pressed himself tight against her, his erection hard against her belly.

And she wanted so much more. She rose on tiptoes, her hands around his neck, and hooked one leg around his hips. She slid her hands down to stroke his heavily muscled backside. He kissed her again and again, his hands exploring. He wasn't heading toward the finish line. He was slow, methodical, and careful. Cherishing her body, needs, and emotions.

When he drew back from his heavy passionate kisses to now trace a line down her throat to her collarbone, his tongue tasting, exploring, and loving, she opened her arms and fell backward on his bed and laid there, her legs wide open and welcoming.

He leaned over her but paused, taking a moment to just stare. "Oh, my God, you're so beautiful."

She shook her head. "As long as you think so."

He bent over, dropping a kiss onto her ribs, his finger stroking down the valleys and hollows of her body. He knelt between her legs, gently cupping her breasts, exploring her belly and long legs, slowly dragging his fingers up the inside of her thighs. He slipped one long finger underneath the edge of the elastic on her white cotton panties, gently stroking, teasing. With his other hand he slipped his fingers into the top, sliding them to the side. She gasped and twisted on the bed.

"You're still wearing too many clothes."

He shifted, then drew her panties down and off. She watched as he stared at her. He swallowed hard. She worried something was wrong, but then he whispered, "And you've got red hair below."

With unexpected movement he slid his fingers through the bright curls and moistness, sliding one finger right inside.

Her hips rose up as she cried out in surprise. Immediately he added a second, gently coaxing.

"Jesus, Rhodes."

And with his thumb he found the tiny nub hidden in her soft folds. She cried out again as he gently teased and tormented her.

She couldn't take too much of that. She wanted him inside her. "Rhodes, come to me," she demanded.

Sienna wrapped her legs tightly around his body, and with powerful thighs, drew him toward her. He slid his hands upward as he licked, leaving a moist pathway on her ribs, stopping to suckle one breast, then moving to latch onto the other nipple, giving it his full attention. By the time he rose up to capture her mouth, she was trembling.

He looked down at her, his hands holding her head in place, his voice as dark as midnight as he whispered, "You're mine."

And he entered her all the way.

Pinned beneath him, she was lost in a fury of sensations as he slowly seated himself deep, then moved inside her. With her long legs wrapped around him as hard and tight as she could, he took her to a place she'd never been—then tossed her off the edge into a kaleidoscope of exploding nerve endings.

Dimly she heard herself cry out, but it was distant, as was the sound of his own as he joined her floating in the cloud of sensation.

Tears tugged at her eyes. Emotions at her heart.

The sense of completeness, oneness, at her soul.

When he slipped to one side, cuddling her close, he whispered against her ear, "Are you okay?"

And she whispered, "Never better."

RHODES TIGHTENED HIS arm around her, a smile on his face. This was an unexpected pleasure. As much as he'd hoped to get here, he hadn't thought to do so this fast. Then again, they'd been dancing around this for weeks. Such a joy to hold her in his arms. She shifted her position slightly, snuggling close.

He should get up and talk to Levi and the others about any further developments. But he didn't want to move. He figured by now somebody would've been alerted to the fact that his door was now closed. He and Sienna would be given some time together, but there was no guarantee of how long. Of course no one would know for sure until he and Sienna showed up, and it was written on their faces.

"I guess we should get up?"

He hugged her gently. "Can't say I want to."

"No, can't say I do either." She puffed out a heavy sigh. "But we should find out if Levi has any news. I'd like to know who attacked you at the gas station."

A laugh rumbled up from his chest. "I'm less concerned about that than I am making sure the Dallas police found the man responsible for the attempted hostage taking."

"Any chance they were the same?"

"Only if it was yet another hired gun. And that's possible."

She raised herself up on her elbow and looked down at him. "What do you mean?"

"If there was one man who hired the attack on the DA's office building, chances are he still had a different person go in and shoot the men in the garage. And that same man could've followed us out of town and attacked me at the gas station."

"But we didn't see anyone tailing us," she said, staring down at him.

"No, but it was a long drive and a lot of traffic."

She sagged back into his arms. "So easy to be a criminal in this world. We make it too easy on them."

"Another reason we're never out of work," Rhodes said quietly. He sat up gently. "Stay here. I'm taking a quick shower." He glanced at his clock and winced. "I'd coax you in there with me but for the time."

She chuckled. "Next time."

He lowered his head and grinned. "Glad to hear there'll be one."

He kissed her with enough passion that her arms snaked around his neck to tug him back into bed. He pulled free and escaped to the bathroom, regret in his heart. *Later.* He'd hold her in his arms all night. That was the only thought which kept him walking in the direction of the bathroom.

Standing under the water a few minutes later, his mind returned to his attacker. Chances were good, if he'd been followed to the gas station, they were all the way to the compound too. He figured Levi and the others would've considered that fact, but it was tearing him up inside and would until he brought it up to them. The last thing they needed was another attack there.

He also needed to contact Robert to see if there was any news on his end and to give him an update. Rhodes's head still ached, but he carefully soaked it under the hot water. Using a bit of shampoo, he cleaned his hair. By the time he was done, dried off and stepped into his bedroom with a towel wrapped around his waist, he found his bed made and Sienna sitting in the chair where she'd been when he'd woken up, now with her laptop open, checking her emails.

And she was fully dressed.

Too bad.

"Find anything?" He leaned over and kissed her on the forehead. She smiled, snagged a hand around his neck and pulled him down for real one. When he finally straightened, his blood was boiling. "Hold that thought," he said, his voice hoarse. Shaking the shreds of passion back to where they belonged, *for now*, he quickly pulled clothes from his dresser and got dressed. Finally he turned around and asked, "You ready?"

She took a deep breath and let it out very slowly. And she grinned. "Sure. What's the worst they can do? Fire me?"

His eyebrows shot up. "We are both consenting adults, and every one of them saw this happening."

She shrugged. "Maybe."

He clasped her hands in his, tugging her forward. "It'll be just fine."

Chapter 15

S HE PLASTERED A smile on her face and asked a question as they approached the kitchen. "Do you think we'll have to go back to Dallas?"

"I doubt it." They walked in, smiled at everybody, and filled two cups of coffee, while still talking. "No need for us to drive up there again."

On that note he turned to face Levi and asked, "Any update?"

Levi shook his head. "Nothing worthwhile." He studied Rhodes and asked, "How you feeling? You took quite a blow to your head."

"It doesn't appear to have broken the skin though, right?" Sienna asked, worriedly studying his head. She turned to look at Ice. "It's just like a concussion, correct?"

More comfortable now, Sienna walked around the table and sat down across from Rhodes, beside Ice.

Sienna looked at Rhodes critically and shrugged. "Obviously whatever it was didn't hold him down too long. If it'd been me who had been hit in the head ..." She shrugged. "I probably wouldn't be awake for days."

Rhodes glared at her. "You *were* hit in the head and knocked unconscious—and I tried to get you to stay in the hospital—remember?"

She winced, feeling foolish, Rhodes's injury having superseded her own. "I … forgot."

"Well, I haven't. And I'll have enough nightmares from that one time already, thank you very much."

She laughed. "I'm not planning on getting kidnapped or hit in the head again anytime soon."

Rhodes turned to look at Levi and Ice. "As we must have been followed to the gas station, and that's where I was attacked, have you considered we could've been all the way here too?"

"Stone is in the control room right now. He's been searching for any kind of traffic or suspicious activity around us."

Rhodes smiled. "I figured you were on it, but because we didn't talk before now, I wasn't sure."

Sienna felt her jaw drop as she glared at him. "And you didn't think to mention that possibility the whole time I drove home?"

"Would it have done any good?" he asked bluntly. "You were doing what you could to get us here. That's what counted. And you were doing a damn good job at it. If we'd needed more support from the team they'd have come and helped us. But we didn't. We were good. *You* were great."

"I just do not think the way you guys do." She slumped back into her chair and rubbed her temple. "I told you I don't do trouble," she wailed.

"Good thing." Ice smiled at her and patted her hand gently. "You went through enough yesterday. The wounded leading the wounded home. We're just grateful you both made it safely here."

"What now then?" Sienna asked. "Did you get to update Bullard?"

"I spoke with him not long ago, told him what happened to you and Rhodes. He's got some men heading over to check the charity run by J. R. Wilson. Bullard says just his check of the exterior of the warehouse is suspicious as hell. And he wants to have a better look."

"Can he do that?" Sienna asked, looking from Levi to Rhodes and back again.

The corner of Levi's mouth kicked up. "This is Bullard we're talking about. And Africa. Although there are rules everywhere, some over there are slightly different. At least for him."

She wondered about that. But Bullard had a lot of connections. And he wasn't green in this field. Whereas she was. She relaxed some at those thoughts.

Lissa walked in just then. She beamed when she saw Sienna and rushed over to hug her. "Oh, my God! Are you feeling okay? I couldn't believe it when Stone told me what happened." She crouched down beside Sienna and gently cupped her cheek. "I'm so sorry this happened to you." And in true Lissa form she wrapped her arms around Sienna and hugged her again.

Sienna pulled back slightly, wondering how she got so lucky as to find not just these men but these women as well. "I'm fine, honest. It was a bit rough yesterday morning. The worst part was, according to Rhodes, the two guys who kidnapped me were young teenage punks and could barely carry me, so they basically dragged me down the stairs. When I woke up, I had more spots that hurt than I thought were possible."

Lissa winced. "That sounds absolutely horrible."

Sienna grinned. "Yeah, that wasn't the highlight of my day. Neither was finding Rhodes knocked out on the ground." She cast a teasing eye across the table. "No way could I lift him. I was ready to call 911 to get somebody to help me load the lug."

Everyone laughed. She looked over at Levi. "Any update on the men who kidnapped me? I understand the attack on the DA's office probably took precedence, but it would be nice to hear of those two men's fates."

"They will be put away for a long time for hurting you," Lissa said loyally. She sneaked into a spot between them, the three women now sitting together.

"Robert said they were still talking, giving up names," Levi told her. "With any luck this issue will be over soon."

"Except for the last guy who killed everybody," she said bitterly. "I'll sleep well tonight if they have number seven in jail too."

"You'll sleep just fine regardless," Rhodes said calmly. "Everyone is out looking for the man. He's got to be on cameras somewhere in the building. They will find him. Don't you worry."

"Except he followed us to the vehicle and gas station."

"But we don't know if it was him or just someone he hired," Levi said.

"So that makes it better?" Sienna slumped in her chair. "That just means there are more assholes out there gunning for us."

"But you're safe here." Alfred walked in then. He took a look at Rhodes and Sienna and said, "Glad to hear you two are back home. If you want to clean off the table, dinner will be ready in about thirty minutes."

Sienna straightened. "Oh, great! I'm famished."

Rhodes laughed. "When are you not?"

Lissa confessed at her side, "I'm looking forward to the next meal too."

Merk called out from the doorway, "Are you ladies ever *not* hungry?"

Sienna grinned at Merk and Katina as they walked in, holding hands. She turned toward Levi and said, "You should change the company name from Heroes for Hire to Heroes from Heaven."

An immediate shocked silence was broken by a giggle, coming from the most unexpected person. Ice couldn't hold back.

Levi stood up, raised his chin and glared at her, but no heat was behind it as he said, "The company's *name* is Legendary Security. The Heroes for Hire was just a nickname. And it sure as hell won't be Heroes from Heaven." He snorted. "Bad enough everybody around here is pairing up. It's like a bloody love nest instead of a compound." And he walked out.

Ice tried to get to her feet, but was laughing too hard. She turned to look at Sienna and said, "Oh, I've wanted to say that for a long time." She reached over and gave Sienna a big hug, "Good for you." Then she got up and followed Levi.

Rhodes shook his head. "That's just demoralizing, that's what that is."

"What, *heroes*?" Sienna asked. "Heroes for Hire makes sense, and you guys bash that name around lots too."

"Yeah, Heroes for the Heart has been mentioned too, but Heroes from Heaven?"

"Well, I think it's a lovely name," Lissa said with a smile. "And I might just keep using it."

"Not if you don't want an all-out war," Rhodes warned. "As a joke that's one thing, but don't ever mean it."

Sienna looked over at him. "I guess this is some kind of an ego thing?"

Lissa looked at him too. "Because Heroes for the Heart sounds lovely too," she said. "You know that, right?"

Stone walked around the table, bent down and kissed her. "You are lovely. But there's no way in hell I would allow a name like that. This is not a romantic retreat here."

Sienna batted her eyes at him. "But it could be."

"Ha." Stone flashed a grin at her. "Not everybody gets to spend the day in bed, you know?" He turned that knowing look on Rhodes before flashing back at her. "Must be nice to have your own hero from heaven." And he headed into the kitchen to give Alfred a hand.

Beside her Lissa giggled. She leaned close to Sienna and whispered, "Don't tell him this, but we spent a lot of days in bed."

The two women chuckled. Rhodes stood up. "Okay, my turn to leave now."

Sienna quickly but gently kicked him under the table. "You can't. You're helping us clean the table and get ready for our meal. Alfred said the food is coming."

She and Lissa both hopped to their feet and cleared the cups and collected the miscellaneous dishes. They walked into the kitchen, loaded the dishwasher and came back with a big white tablecloth.

By the time the table was set, Alfred brought out the food. The rest of the gang slowly drifted back into the room. Nothing like a meal to bring a family together. And she realized that was what this really was. And she was so blessed to have joined it.

WHEN HE LEFT the military, Rhodes hadn't expected to end up in a scenario like this. The men he worked with here were his family. They'd been brothers in arms in the military and best friends. Ice had naturally joined them, and Rhodes had never felt like he was losing any part of Levi because of his relationship with Ice. And as they'd all slowly come together with their own partners, Rhodes realized just how special this truly was. With the increasing number they had here to actually maintain a positive happy family, well, it was something out of his experience.

What would it be like to have their numbers grow further? There were other men, like Logan and Harrison, who had moved into the compound and who knew if Flynn would as well. He'd done well protecting Anna and her animal shelter when he'd been given the chance. The team had discussed Flynn's execution of that job, and it had been a group decision to bring him on board. Flynn was a character, and Rhodes looked forward to seeing him again, and Rhodes was also dying to meet Anna, as Flynn had a lot to say about her. The last words out of his mouth on the issue had been, "Good riddance."

Katina, who'd overheard Rhodes laughing at Flynn, instead of being upset, had just said, "It'd be interesting to get Anna's take on this."

Maybe they would now. As Katina was hoping to have her friend visit her at the compound.

Rhodes suspected Flynn wasn't anywhere near as untouched by the Anna experience as he tried to make it sound. And Rhodes had to admit that finding Sienna made him want the same opportunity for all his buddies.

Alfred sat down at the head of the table as always, with Levi at the other end, and said, "Bon appétit."

They all dug in. Rhodes didn't know what the name for this concoction was, but it was meat and vegetables smothered in one huge flaky pastry, and it was freaking delicious.

"Bullard phoned," Levi said when everyone had refilled their plates and sat back down again. "They're going into the warehouse tonight."

Silence. Rhodes glanced over at him and said, "Wish I was there."

"He'll go in with a tactical team and will let us know what they find."

"I'm surprised it wasn't some kind of joint effort with us."

"If we had confirmation they were the ones responsible for the goings-on here, then it would have been. But we don't have that yet."

Rhodes glanced at Sienna to see her gaze down on her plate. "It'll be fine," he reassured her.

She lifted her face to his, then swept her gaze over all the people seated at the table and said, "These men are killers. One got away, and we know the charity has offices in Dallas. Is there no way to see what they're doing here?"

Rhodes caught Levi's look as he studied her. He chewed methodically as they all considered the issue. "Find proof they are involved, then we can."

She stared directly at Levi for a long moment. Then nodded. "I'll work on that after dinner."

Rhodes turned to look at her, a question in his eyes. But he thought better of it. Maybe she had a few tricks up her sleeve they didn't know about. He was willing to give her the benefit of the doubt. Maybe she was just reaching, hoping she could find something to put this nightmare to rest. For that he couldn't blame her.

Chapter 16

AFTER DINNER, SIENNA grabbed a cup of coffee and made her way back to her desk in the office. It was late; she was tired, but her mind buzzed. Surely there was more information to find. With no one around to hear her, she freely talked to herself out loud. And that made her feel better as she went over what she knew so far.

She brought up her notes on her laptop, refreshed the page, then walked to the table where the spreadsheets still lay. Pulling up a chair she grabbed a blank notepad and emptied her mind. She studied the number and letter combinations. It might be names and numbers, but there had to be more to be found here. It would help if she had more sheets, with more data and options, easier to confirm too, because she'd have a larger sample to work with. She took the complex number and letter combinations and wrote down the information she had already decoded with the letters on the side. Then she took a look at the numbers lined up. Was it also in a pattern, or were they something simpler? Like an invoice number, purchase dates, or could they be random? "No, not random," she whispered. "It's too specific to be."

There had to be a pattern. It didn't mean she would know what it was. Then she turned to look at the spreadsheets Bullard had sent. These papers had been found in the young IT guy's desk. She'd started with the first but hadn't caught anything. Just more numbers. This time just straight numbers and columns. The final column appeared to be monetary amounts—a decimal point two digits in from the right. But no dollar sign. And for this level she doubted anybody dealt in change. But accountants the world over kept precise track of every transaction. She put that page down and picked up another.

By the time she had the third one, an idea sparked in the back of her mind. She grabbed her notepad and tossed around codes, numbers, and ideas. Finally she sat back and noticed it had been over two hours, and she had a glimmer of truth in her hand. But she needed Bullard to confirm. She also needed to review the names she had gathered so far, including the six dead gunmen.

She got up and walked back to her laptop. She'd noted the various people her decoding had brought up. She added the six people from the shooting in Dallas, wondering if she should pull up Robert's name too.

She went back to the spreadsheets, checked every one that had an R.F., considering the numbers behind it. If he was involved—and that was a small *if*—he was the only one she knew of who might confirm some of these numbers.

What if these were bank accounts? What if they were payments into one with his name on it? She had several from the Swiss bank.

Back at her laptop again she printed off every Swiss bank account. Then with a highlighter, she quickly cross-checked them and found nothing. Now that was wrong. She knew something had to be here; she could feel it. And then she saw it. In an attempt to confuse the account numbers, the first and last characters had been switched. And with that knowledge, she quickly decoded all the bank account numbers in front of the initials. Now she needed somebody to confirm the name on these accounts.

"This is it," she said jubilantly.

"This is what?" Rhodes asked.

Surprised, she looked up to see him leaning against the doorjamb, watching her.

"I think I solved it."

He came around to look at the data she had.

She quickly showed him how the accounts unscrambled onto the scanned ledger sheets with the ripped edges. "I think these are the accounts and names they belong to." She sat back. "And I can't let go of the idea that R.F. is Robert Forrest, the DA."

Rhodes shook his head. "No, I don't think so. R.F. could mean a lot of people. He'd been with us. He had ample opportunity to set us up or to get rid of us himself."

She frowned. "That's true," she said slowly. "And if he had hired somebody to go in the building when we were there, it would've been a simple enough case to have taken us out. He had a cell phone with him." She shrugged. "I wasn't making him be the bad guy. I was just fitting the name to the R.F. initials."

"*Robert* is only one of the many possibilities."

She nodded. "And that takes us down a rabbit hole because there's probably hundreds, if not thousands, of potential combinations."

"Hundreds of thousands." He tapped the papers on the table. "But this is interesting, and very good." He glanced down at her. "We can ask Bullard if he knows any of these people on his end. And we can also get somebody here on ours, someone a little higher up, to help us out and get some names for these accounts."

"In fact, that is something Robert could probably do for us, right?" she asked drily. She glanced down at her watch. "It's seven. Probably too late to call him now."

Rhodes laughed. "We could certainly email him. If he's working, then he'll be on it and answer pretty fast."

With him sitting beside her, she quickly typed up an email, documenting bits and pieces that she'd found. She hit Send.

He held out a hand and asked, "You ready to leave the office now?"

Her laptop dinged immediately. She sat back down and looked. "It's Robert."

She heard Rhodes's heavy sigh beside her and realized he probably had different plans for her this evening than what she was currently doing. She smiled. Now *that* she could get behind. Still ... "Let me just see what he says."

She brought up his email in response. There were only two words, *thank you*. She sat back, stared at them and shrugged. "Just because I'm excited about it, doesn't mean anybody else is."

He chuckled. "And Robert is probably way too tired to deal with any of this."

She winced. "I had to stay behind and handle a lot of late nights in my former position, so I understand how overwhelming it can be." She sat there and stared at the thank you for a long moment. She didn't like it.

"I haven't had any contact or dealings with him in the past, but this seems way too simplistic for an email from him. And no capitals."

He stopped and stared at her. "What are you talking about?"

She shrugged. "I asked a bunch of questions, gave a lot of information." She turned her gaze to him and asked, "And all he says is 'thank you'?"

She scrolled down to his signature, just below the message. And above the signature was an odd series of digits, numbers. She sat back and said, "Whoa."

He walked around and asked, "What?"

She pointed out the code on the bottom. "This helps." She turned to gaze up at him. "It's the same code I had explained to him earlier on the accounts."

He stared at her, then the email, pulled out his phone and tried to phone Robert. She waited in her seat, studying the code, her blood running hot at the thought of somebody going after the Dallas DA. But of course, that could've been because they'd gone after Rhodes and her.

"Why didn't we check on him before?" Her body was tense as she waited for Robert to pick up his phone.

But his phone rang and rang. Finally it went to voicemail. Rhodes didn't leave a message. He turned it off and said, "I'll find Levi."

She closed her laptop, tucked it under her arm and raced behind him. "Any idea where they are?"

"Last I heard, they were talking with Alfred in the kitchen area." They ran down the stairs and burst into the kitchen. All three people turned to look at them.

"What's up?" barked Levi.

Sienna opened the laptop, hit the button to bring it out of screensaver mode and showed him the email with the little bit of code on the bottom. "If I decode this like for the other accounts to get names," she said, "that particular line of code reads *help me*."

THE DISCUSSION WAS hot and heavy as they decided the best way forward. Harrison came in from the other room where he was watching a movie, snagged up the laptop with Sienna's permission and checked to see where the message came from.

"It was sent from his house," he announced ten minutes later. But he glanced at his watch.

"That's ... several hours' drive away," Sienna said. "We should call the cops and have them go by his house."

Ice said, "We already contacted somebody there. But they'll check first if he's being held hostage. If they just knock on the door, there's a good chance they won't find out anything or will get a bullet through the door themselves."

Rhodes knew the truth was hard sometimes, but Sienna needed to understand these people were dead serious and had long-reaching arms.

Levi's phone rang. He pulled it out and said, "It's Robert." He waited a second for silence to follow, then held it to his ear and asked, "Hello, Robert, that you?"

Rhodes watched Levi's face as his gaze hardened. It zinged to Sienna and if possible, became even harder.

"I heard you. Where do you want to make the exchange?" He turned and faced Ice. "You are where? Almost in Houston?"

Rhodes waited and realized exactly what was happening. He checked his watch, mentally ran over the weapons they had ready and the men available. The plan of action would be determined by wherever the exchange was because Rhodes had no doubt they had Robert and were looking for Sienna too. Levi would have said, *in exchange*, but in reality, one of them was likely already dead. Which meant they were all leaving and Sienna would stay here, where she'd be safe.

Levi closed the phone. "A hotel on the other side of Houston. They've come into our neck of the woods. An hour." He stared at everybody at the table. "This will take every one of us. We're to meet in the parking lot."

Rhodes pursed his lips. "That's still pretty public."

Harrison snapped, "Even worse, he could have a dozen men hiding inside the hotel rooms with sniper rifles already in position now."

Levi nodded. "He said Rhodes must come too."

Rhodes crossed his arms over his chest and said, "I wouldn't have it any other way."

"No way you're going," cried Sienna. "He wants to kill you."

Rhodes turned to stare at her. "No way in hell you are."

She stuck her chin out at him and said, "We have to stop them and help Robert. These bad guys think they can just take out a DA now?"

"Five minutes ago you thought that DA might *be* the bad guy," Rhodes said calmly. "And you're not leaving. You're safe here. That's the way you'll stay."

"And no way are we getting Robert back if they don't see me there." She added in a low voice, "Or you, for that matter."

He opened his mouth to order her to stay when Levi stepped in.

"You know she's right, Rhodes. She has to be visible— not accessible. We can protect her. But we have to do this. We'll need all hands."

"One hour's not much time." Rhodes stood up. "We must get there earlier and park somewhere else."

"We need a plan," Ice said as she stood up, facing them. "I can fly several into town but where to land and have wheels there?"

Levi studied her. "If we take the helicopter, we're likely to trigger an alarm, and it's not worth it. We'll be faster driving. It's only thirty minutes out."

"We do need a plan," Rhodes snapped. "But let's make it while we're driving. Because there's just no time otherwise."

"We'll take three vehicles," Levi said, standing up. "Everybody gear up. This could get ugly so come fully armed. Ice with me, Sienna with Rhodes."

Stone walked in just then and asked, "Do you want to leave somebody here or not?"

"I'll stay," Alfred said. "I'll be in the control room with Lissa and Katina." He nodded to the women. "Sienna has to go. Otherwise, I would have kept her here too."

"We leave in five."

The room scattered.

Rhodes kept his gaze on Sienna. She clenched the laptop, her knuckles white. He told her, "Grab a sweater. Don't know how late this night'll be. We'll take the same truck as the last time. Be there in five." He waited, watched her nod before she bolted from the room. He turned back to Alfred and the other two women. "Use the satellite and see if you can find the hotel. You start searching now, you might be able to give us the heads-up as to what is waiting for us."

"We'll be up there in five minutes. As soon as you're all off the compound, we're in lockdown."

Rhodes gave him a curt nod and headed to the truck. On the way, he stopped at the weapons room. They had depots all around the compound with a full armory downstairs. He pulled out several handguns and put one into his shoulder holster, then tucked a spare in his ankle boot.

He grabbed the keys and raced to the truck. Now all he needed was Sienna and they were gone. As he shifted the truck into Reverse to back up, the passenger door opened, and Sienna hopped in.

She quickly buckled up and said, "Let's go."

She slammed the door shut; he hit the power locks and ripped out of the compound. Levi drove with Ice, Harrison rode in the back. Stone drove the third truck carrying Merk. The full team.

Every one of them ready to kick some ass.

Chapter 17

THE TRIP WAS fast and furious and done almost in complete silence. At least for the first five minutes. Then Sienna ran communications between Ice and Rhodes. By the time they hit the outskirts of the city, the plan was for Levi's team to meet up two blocks on the other side of the hotel. They were running ten minutes early as Rhodes pulled in to rendezvous with Levi and the others. Rhodes grabbed his phone and called Alfred. "What did you see?"

Rhodes held the phone slightly away from his ear so Sienna could hear.

"Two snipers, one each top right second floor and top left third."

She stared at Rhodes in horror.

"What's in the parking lot?"

"One dark sedan," Alfred said. "Quite possibly belongs to Robert himself."

"Did you recognize any faces?" Rhodes asked.

"No. But we're running what we have through facial recognition. Can't get decent images yet."

"Okay, we're a couple blocks away, about to set plans into motion." He turned to stare out the window.

"One more thing," Alfred continued. "Bullard checked in. Warehouse was full of weapons. He sent a warning. Now that the cache has been seized, the police are all over J. R.

Wilson's ass." He paused. "In other words these men are prepared to do anything to get away."

"Got it. We'll call with an update as soon as we can. Record everything, will you?" He pocketed his phone, turned to look at Sienna and asked, "You ready?"

She let her breath rush out and said, "At least for this part."

The plan was simple. The other two vehicles would park here, and the men would take positions inside and out of the hotel. Levi, Rhodes, and Sienna would appear for the meeting. Simple with not a whole lot of options. Only this time they were going in Levi's truck, just the three of them driving in to the hotel parking lot. She stared down at her hands, not surprised to see the fine tremor working its way through her fingers. This was not exactly how she'd expected to spend her evening. She just hoped to hell there would be a night after, not the endless one she suspected was the plan for her.

She ran her fingers over her face to still the panic erupting inside. They all had weapons, and for the first time, she wondered if she'd rather have one too. She was completely defenseless. She understood the risks of arming an untrained person. Maybe Rhodes would teach her. She really didn't want to be in this kind of situation again and not have any skills. She knew Ice was hell on wheels with many weapons. Wouldn't it be nice if Sienna could at least learn some of that?

Also, considering her free time while living and working at the compound, maybe she could convince somebody to give her some martial arts practice—something she'd really like to get back to. Maybe she hadn't forgotten all of it. Surely if she got into a wrestling match with these guys, it would come back to her.

The vehicle was parked in front of the hotel as they had been told. Levi drove around until he was facing back out again, and pulled up at a cross angle to the vehicle.

Nobody moved.

"Do I get out?" Sienna asked in a low voice.

"Not yet. Wait until we see Robert, alive."

The passenger and driver side doors of the sedan opened. The man on the far side got out first. She didn't recognize him. The driver hopped out, and she didn't recognize him either. They were followed by two more muscle men.

Then the rear passenger door was opened on the far side. Robert got out. A very disabled, bloodied Robert. She caught back her small cry. "Oh, my God. Did they have to hurt him like that?" She opened her door and stepped out.

And then she stopped when she saw the man walking toward her. "Bobby?" She stared at the man who'd brought her coffee, delivered her the printer she needed, and anything else for those hours she'd been at the DA's office. And something else clicked. *Bobby was short for Robert*, and she sighed. "R.F. by any chance?"

He looked at her in confusion. "What are you talking about?

"Your last name, does it start with an *F*?" she snapped as she walked toward them.

Rhodes walked at her side, his arm holding her back. She could feel her anger rising inside. These bullies with a need to inflict pain on everybody had to be taken down.

Bobby frowned and replied, "Yes, but how the hell would you know that?"

She snorted. "You really are stupid, aren't you? Did you have to hurt Robert? Did you break his bones just for your own satisfaction?"

"I had to do what I had to do. With Wilson's operation now compromised, and you two meddling into things, I had to make a run for it. The gunrunning was a great way to make cash. The drugs were ugly but necessary. I've wanted to get out for a long time. Now I have to. The only way to do that is to make sure I don't leave any threads behind. And that means the three of you."

"Sorry for upsetting your plans." She gave him a saccharine smile to let him know she was anything but. In truth, she wanted to reach out and smack him, but Rhodes was being very particular about keeping her at his side. She didn't understand why, but he was too strong for her to argue with. She shot him a harsh look as if to tell him to leave her alone. She had another question for Bobby. "How did you lose the pages to the ledger?"

"Shut up, bitch. You think you're so smart, but that had nothing to do with me. Goddamn J. R. Wilson. He didn't even notice after a meeting at the bank in Africa. That man's a mess. That stupid IT kid ripped out the ledger pages, then tried to blackmail us. We didn't even have a solution worked out for him yet. Hopefully you'll nail his ass to the wall too," Bobby snapped. "Not that it matters to you. You don't know anything."

He raised his hand to the sky, instinctively she ducked.

And he dropped his arm as if he were starting a race.

Rhodes held her tight against him. And she realized he'd been expecting snipers to fire. She straightened and faced Bobby. With more bravado than she felt, she sneered. "What exactly is that surprise you've got for me?"

He glared at her, raised his arm and dropped it once more.

Nothing happened.

"Missing something?" Rhodes asked.

Levi, now standing on the other side of Sienna, said, "We thought we'd even the odds and take out your snipers."

Bobby's face hardened into a cruel laugh. "You didn't think I came with just those two, did you?"

Instantly gunfire erupted all around them.

Rhodes grabbed Sienna and tucked her behind the truck. She dropped to the ground instinctively.

"Roll under," Rhodes ordered as he pulled out a gun and fired over the truck bed. Shots came from the left and behind.

"Shit."

She twisted underneath the truck to look at him. "Rhodes, you hurt?"

He shifted into a squatting position and fired again.

"Stop right there," Bobby snapped in a hard voice. And he had a rifle aimed right at Rhodes's back.

"Stand up slowly and throw the gun on the ground."

Shit! ... She didn't know what she should do. She watched as Rhodes slowly straightened. All around them the gunfire slowed down.

Levi yelled out, "Leave my men alone, and I'll leave yours alone."

"Like hell. This is the asshole who knocked out my men in the garage. I had to shoot them because of him."

Rhodes snorted. "You were just looking for an excuse to kill them anyway."

"They were sloppy. Stupidly so." The rifle butt jammed in Rhodes's back this time, making him gasp.

And that was when she saw the gun tucked into Rhodes's boot. His pant leg was caught over the top of it.

But Bobby didn't know. She heard him say something else but her gaze was on that handle. Her hand snaked out, lifted the gun free. She was under the truck, no one the wiser. *Yet.*

Except for Rhodes. He knew what she'd done.

She stared at the gun in her hand.

Beside the truck, so close to her, Bobby said, "Get down on your knees, asshole."

She watched as Rhodes slowly lowered to the ground beside her. And realized she didn't have time for decisions here. She flipped sideways so she could see the man, lifted the gun and pointed at his chest.

Then pulled the trigger.

The sound of the gun firing echoed in the silence.

For a long moment no one moved. Bobby slowly sank to his knees and fell over sideways. Rhodes spun, kicked the gun away from the man, then turned and dragged her out from under the truck, pulling her to her feet. He grabbed her, held her tight against him and whispered against her ear, "Thank God, you're safe."

She threw her arms around his neck and held him close. "You mean, thank God, you're safe." With a half laugh, she pulled back, placed her hands on his cheeks and kissed him hard. "When he put that gun to your back and told you to go down on your knees ..." She kissed him again. "I was so scared."

He stepped back and glared at her. "What were you thinking?"

She laughed. "That I didn't want to lose you." And she again hugged him tight. Over her shoulder she could see Levi, standing guard on two other men. The two other compound vehicles raced in and came to a sudden stop. Everybody hopped out.

Ice raced over to Robert, leaning against the car. She had her med kit with her but called out, "Somebody call 911. Robert needs an ambulance now."

Not that they needed to worry. All the gunshots had alerted somebody. Sirens already raced toward them. But that would be the cops, and they needed medical help for Robert. Sienna pulled out her phone and quickly dialed it in. She patted Rhodes on the shoulder and walked over to help Ice. She crouched down in front of Robert, now lying on the ground with Ice beside him.

"Robert, how you feeling?"

He rolled his head to look at her and said, "You got my message, I see."

"I did. But this asshole phoned Levi anyway within a few minutes. Still, you gave us just that much of a warning."

He closed his eyes. "Good. I worked with Bobby for ten years. Ten long years and I had no idea."

"When you're back on your feet, you can rip his sorry life apart. He's dead, so he won't be going to jail. But a lot of other people were involved in this mess. Like J. R. Wilson. Bobby's statement should help to nail his ass to the wall."

Robert gave a broken laugh. "I can't wait."

Rhodes came and collected Sienna as the cops came roaring into the parking lot. Levi stepped forward and quickly explained the issue. Including the identification of Robert as the Dallas DA. At his name the place erupted into organized chaos.

The ambulance arrived five minutes later. While she watched, Robert was quickly loaded into the back of the vehicle and driven off. She turned to face Rhodes. "Should somebody go with him?"

Rhodes shook his head. "I believe he has a married

daughter in this area. The police will be calling her. She'll likely make it to the hospital shortly after the ambulance."

Sienna said, "I hope so. At times like this, nobody should be alone."

The last thing she wanted was for the man who'd done so much for his city to recuperate on his own. As she glanced back at the cops all around the place, she realized it would be another long night. "I guess there's no chance in hell we'll get to bed anytime soon, is there?"

"Nope. It'll be a while."

AND HE WAS right. It was. But it could've been so much worse. Still, it was another three hours before they drove into the compound once again. Alfred and the other two women met them at the door.

Alfred took one look and said, "To bed, all of you."

Rhodes wouldn't argue with that. He was beat. But he made sure he didn't go alone. He grabbed Sienna's hand and headed for the elevator. At his suite, he didn't even give her a chance to comment as he dragged her inside. He closed and locked the door and said, "Sleep. All I need is sleep."

She stood in the middle of the room and watched as he stripped down and collapsed on his side of the bed. She took off her clothes, tossed them on the floor and crawled into bed beside him. He lay there, resting. She reached up and kissed him. "Thank you for being you."

His eyes popped open. "You're welcome, but that's a very interesting thing to say. I'm nobody special. I'm just me."

"That's not true. You're a hero to me."

He winced. "Remember, we don't use that word."

196

She reached up and placed a finger across his lips. "Levi can say whatever he wants. But for me, you're my hero and always will be." She threw her arms around him and kissed him hard, pressing her breasts against him, her hips cuddling his growing erection.

When he finally came up for air, he brushed his nose against hers, his heart swelling with an emotion he barely recognized. "Have I told you that I love you?"

Her gaze widened in delight. She shook her head. "No, you haven't. But it's a damn good thing because I love you too."

Their gazes locked and slowly he turned his head, his warm breath washing over her as he whispered, "Maybe I was a little too quick to say I needed sleep."

His hand slid down her back to cup her butt and tug her hard against him. "I think sleep can wait a little longer."

And he lowered his head and kissed her, knowing for the first time what it was to make love to the woman he loved. He was a one-woman man, and Sienna was his. Forever.

Epilogue

"HEY, ANNA," FLYNN Kilpatrick said as he walked up to the pallet of dog food she was unloading. "I just came from Levi's compound. Figured, since I was in town, I'd give you the good news in person."

She straightened, brushed the hair back off her face. "Hi. That's a crazy place to be these days. Katina told me about Rhodes and Sienna. I'm going down there this afternoon if I can get away."

"Good." He reached down and hefted several bags over his shoulder, walking inside to stack them in the shed. "But I wanted to tell you that the last of the men involved in Katina's kidnapping have been locked up. We heard this morning. Even better, several are talking, and the DA is expecting everyone to go away for a very long time."

"Great," she said with a big smile. "I'm so happy to hear that. I'd hate to have anything else bad happen to Katina."

"Merk won't allow it." He grinned at her. "Looks like the two of them are fairly matched up."

"They matched up a long time ago. They are just now realizing how perfect they are together."

Flynn laughed. Anna had told him a little bit about Merk and Katina's relationship. He'd heard the rest from the guys. It was all good. As a matter of fact, it was looking damn rosy around the compound. He'd been there just this morning. He heard about all the chaos with Rhodes and Sienna. But he'd been out on the West Coast with Logan on a short job for Levi and had missed all the fun. Typical. But damn. Rhodes and Sienna—who knew they were a thing?

"That is great. Thanks for stopping by," she said. "I know how much you were hoping to get hired into the company."

He was indeed. And this next job would be short and sweet. With any luck he'd get over to Saudi Arabia, handle this problem and get back home again. The timeline was tight, but that was the way they liked it. And he wasn't going alone; his buddies—Logan and Harrison, were going. That worked for him. He'd left his jacket at Anna's to give him a reason to come back. But as the good news had come in, he hadn't needed it – this time. Now he had an excuse to stop by after his next trip.

He wondered if she'd seen it. He'd hung it on the back of the door. Hopefully obvious enough for a man to see and understand but not so obvious that Anna would see.

He brushed the dirt off his hands, checked out the shed's roof and realized the dog food would be nice and dry here. He closed the door, snapped the simple lock closed. Then he picked up the empty pallet, moved it to the stack with the others behind the shed. "Anything else?"

She shook her head but kept her face away from him. "That's it. Thanks for the help." Her voice was overly cheerful and bright as she turned to face him with a big smile. "I appreciate your timing for a visit. I have to admit, it was great to have your muscles for the couple weeks you were here. This last week, well, I missed that."

"You need to get yourself an assistant. You know that, right?"

She laughed. "I need a lot of things. But it all takes money."

He nodded. "Just don't be thinking about hiring that Jonas character."

She glared at him. "You won't be telling me what to do any longer, thanks. You can leave again now." It was said in a joking manner. They'd done a round or two about Jonas, a guy who kept coming on to her.

"I can't believe you actually dated that guy."

"It was hardly a date. I ran into him at the mall, sat down and had a coffee with him," she protested.

"In Jonas's mind that was a date. Obviously, as he's come around, what? Five times since I've been here? He's bad news. Stay away from him."

"He's not that bad."

"He's worse," Flynn countered. For the weeks while Flynn had been guarding over her, he'd watched her, lived with her, inhaling the scent that was so Anna. And not touching her. But now he was leaving. But not without a taste of her. Especially when he wanted so much more ...

Before she had a chance to protest he tugged her into his arms and said, "There's really only one way to say good-bye." And he lowered his head and kissed her.

Only neither expected the flash of passion that threatened to consume them both. Fireworks exploded in his head. And damn if he didn't hear music.

Anna broke away, gave him an uncertain look, then headed inside her house.

Leaving Flynn wondering what the hell just happened.

This concludes Book 4 of Heroes for Hire: Rhodes's Reward.

Read about Flynn's Firecracker: Heroes for Hire, Book 5

Heroes for Hire: Flynn's Firecracker (Book #5)

Some jobs are a breeze, others are a bitch…

As a trial run that could potentially lead to more work, Flynn agrees to do a security operation for Levi at Legendary Securities. Looking after Anna and her animal shelter should be the easiest job he's ever taken. He doesn't expect the trouble to start when he leaves, job done, and realizes he never wants to leave Anna again.

For Anna, having Flynn around was both a blessing and a curse. She'd enjoyed the help around the extremely large shelter…but every moment they spent together had sparks of wildfire ricocheting between them. Even as she tries to convince herself she's relieved to finally see the (albeit sexy) back of him, he's monopolizing her thoughts again long before she stumbles over the dead body.

Someone is after Flynn, someone who saw Anna and Flynn together, saw the red-hot attraction…and now knows exactly how to get what he wants from his target.

Book 5 is available now!

To find out more visit Dale Mayer's website.

http://smarturl.it/DaleFlynn

Author's Note

Thank you for reading Rhodes's Reward: Heroes for Hire, Book 4! If you enjoyed the book, please take a moment and leave a short review.

Dear reader,

I love to hear from readers, and you can contact me at my website: www.dalemayer.com or at my Facebook author page. To be informed of new releases and special offers, sign up for my newsletter or follow me on BookBub. And if you are interested in joining Dale Mayer's Reader Group, here is the Facebook sign up page.
facebook.com/groups/402384989872660

Cheers,
Dale Mayer

Your THREE Free Books
Are Waiting!

Grab your copy of SEALs of Honor Books 1 – 3 for free!

Meet Mason, Hawk and Dane. *Brave, badass warriors who serve their country with honor and love their women to the limits of life and death.*

DOWNLOAD your copy right now! Just tell me where to send it.
www.smarturl.it/DaleHonorFreeBundle

About the Author

Dale Mayer is a USA Today bestselling author best known for her Psychic Visions and Family Blood Ties series. Her contemporary romances are raw and full of passion and emotion (Second Chances, SKIN), her thrillers will keep you guessing (By Death series), and her romantic comedies will keep you giggling (It's a Dog's Life and Charmin Marvin Romantic Comedy series).

She honors the stories that come to her – and some of them are crazy and break all the rules and cross multiple genres!

To go with her fiction, she also writes nonfiction in many different fields with books available on resume writing, companion gardening and the US mortgage system. She has recently published her Career Essentials Series. All her books are available in print and ebook format.

Connect with Dale Mayer Online

Dale's Website – www.dalemayer.com
Twitter – @DaleMayer
Facebook – dalemayer.com/fb
BookBub – bookbub.com/authors/dale-mayer

Also by Dale Mayer

Published Adult Books:

The K9 Files
Ethan, Book 1
Pierce, Book 2

Lovely Lethal Gardens
Arsenic in the Azaleas, Book 1
Bones in the Begonias, Book 2
Corpse in the Carnations, Book 3
Daggers in the Dahlias, Book 4
Evidence in the Echinacea, Book 5
Footprints in the Ferns, Book 6

Psychic Vision Series
Tuesday's Child
Hide 'n Go Seek
Maddy's Floor
Garden of Sorrow
Knock Knock…
Rare Find
Eyes to the Soul
Now You See Her
Shattered

Into the Abyss

Seeds of Malice

Eye of the Falcon

Itsy-Bitsy Spider

Unmasked

Deep Beneath

Psychic Visions Books 1–3

Psychic Visions Books 4–6

Psychic Visions Books 7–9

By Death Series

Touched by Death

Haunted by Death

Chilled by Death

By Death Books 1–3

Broken Protocols – Romantic Comedy Series

Cat's Meow

Cat's Pajamas

Cat's Cradle

Cat's Claus

Broken Protocols 1-4

Broken and... Mending

Skin

Scars

Scales (of Justice)

Broken but... Mending 1-3

Glory

Genesis

Tori

Celeste

Glory Trilogy

Biker Blues

Morgan: Biker Blues, Volume 1

Cash: Biker Blues, Volume 2

SEALs of Honor

Mason: SEALs of Honor, Book 1

Hawk: SEALs of Honor, Book 2

Dane: SEALs of Honor, Book 3

Swede: SEALs of Honor, Book 4

Shadow: SEALs of Honor, Book 5

Cooper: SEALs of Honor, Book 6

Markus: SEALs of Honor, Book 7

Evan: SEALs of Honor, Book 8

Mason's Wish: SEALs of Honor, Book 9

Chase: SEALs of Honor, Book 10

Brett: SEALs of Honor, Book 11

Devlin: SEALs of Honor, Book 12

Easton: SEALs of Honor, Book 13

Ryder: SEALs of Honor, Book 14

Macklin: SEALs of Honor, Book 15

Corey: SEALs of Honor, Book 16

Warrick: SEALs of Honor, Book 17

Tanner: SEALs of Honor, Book 18

Heroes for Hire

Dezi's Diamond: Heroes for Hire, Book 18

Vince's Vixen: Heroes for Hire, Book 19

Heroes for Hire, Books 1–3

Heroes for Hire, Books 4–6

Heroes for Hire, Books 7–9

Heroes for Hire, Books 10–12

Heroes for Hire, Books 13–15

SEALs of Steel

Badger: SEALs of Steel, Book 1

Erick: SEALs of Steel, Book 2

Cade: SEALs of Steel, Book 3

Talon: SEALs of Steel, Book 4

Laszlo: SEALs of Steel, Book 5

Geir: SEALs of Steel, Book 6

Jager: SEALs of Steel, Book 7

The Final Reveal: SEALs of Steel, Book 8

SEALs of Steel, Books 1–4

SEALs of Steel, Books 5–8

SEALs of Steel, Books 1–8

Collections

Dare to Be You…

Dare to Love…

Dare to be Strong…

RomanceX3

Standalone Novellas

It's a Dog's Life

215

Riana's Revenge

Second Chances

Published Young Adult Books:

Family Blood Ties Series

Vampire in Denial

Vampire in Distress

Vampire in Design

Vampire in Deceit

Vampire in Defiance

Vampire in Conflict

Vampire in Chaos

Vampire in Crisis

Vampire in Control

Vampire in Charge

Family Blood Ties Set 1–3

Family Blood Ties Set 1–5

Family Blood Ties Set 4–6

Family Blood Ties Set 7–9

Sian's Solution, A Family Blood Ties Series Prequel
    Novelette

Design series

Dangerous Designs

Deadly Designs

Darkest Designs

Design Series Trilogy

Standalone

In Cassie's Corner

Gem Stone (a Gemma Stone Mystery)

Time Thieves

Published Non-Fiction Books:

Career Essentials

Career Essentials: The Résumé

Career Essentials: The Cover Letter

Career Essentials: The Interview

Career Essentials: 3 in 1

Printed in Great Britain
by Amazon

55727070R00129